A Dream Away

by
frank drury

This novel is a work of fiction. Names, characters, places and incidents are either the product of the author's imagination or are used fictitiously. Any resemblance to actual events or locales or persons, living or dead, is entirely coincidental.

Printed by CREATESPACE

ISBN-13: 9781461120940
ISBN-10: 1461120942
www.frankdrury.com

Dedicated to my loving wife Lisa and my children Jackson, Jenna, Dana, and Taylor

CHAPTER 1

Two and a Half Men was coming on tonight, which meant he would get lots of good laughs, which he needed, and when it was over he would feel just a little bit better about life. Didn't take much anymore.

After a busy day of trading the markets, Dobs was relieved that the day was over. He had done well, but he was glad it was over. He poured himself a second scotch halfway through the show and finished it just as the show was ending. Drifting off to sleep in his brown leather recliner, he began to remember a time from over thirty years ago when he, like Charlie Harper on the show, thought he had the world by the balls.

He was driving his bright yellow Camaro convertible down Sunset Boulevard when he first arrived in Los

Angeles back in 1975, utterly confident that he would be rich and famous one day. He would sell one of his scripts to a big producer and Jack Nicholson would have the lead role in the film. There was little, if any, doubt in his mind about it.

As soon as he found an apartment he would begin working on it. Anticipating that he would love the next complex he was about to visit, he took a quick turn off of Sunset on to La Cienega and drove about a mile until he saw the signs for the Las Flores Apartments. He pulled in and parked next to the sign that said "Visitor Parking Only." He got out of the car and looked around as he took a deep breath and first became aware of the eucalyptus that hung in the air on this hot July afternoon.

Inside the manager's office he was met by Julie, cute but a little overweight. She was in her mid-thirties and still "waiting for a call" while she passed her time working as an assistant manager of Las Flores. She had dark brown hair and a pretty face that must have been even prettier a few years earlier. Looking into her eyes as he introduced himself, he could see her get turned up a notch as he told her he was a screenwriter. "I am Bill Dobson, a screenwriter. I'm looking for a place to live that offers more inspiration than my old place did."

"And where was your old place, Bill?" she asked curiously.

"Call me Dobs," he told her, "everyone does. I was up in San Francisco, Nob Hill. Had to get out of there. Time to leave, if you know what I mean. So have you been in anything I might have seen?"

He could tell she was somewhat flattered by such a common come-on question as she quickly answered with another standard line, "Just a few soaps so far, but I am expecting a call."

"Super," Dobs responded. "Show me one of these units while we wait."

Julie smiled a great smile back to him, grabbed some keys off the desk, and they were on their way to the model apartment. As he walked along the hot white pavement next to her, he drew back a bit to get a nice glimpse of her ass and he smiled good naturedly when she looked back his way, as though she knew what he was doing and didn't mind at all. "Where are you originally from, Dobs?"

"Oh, I've been in California almost ten years. Came out here from Florida in 1967, part of the hippie movement, and I stayed. How about you?" He looked right into her eyes.

"Been out here my whole life. San Diego born and raised. Dad was in the Navy." She moved with more grace than one would think she would as they turned down a sidewalk and came to the front door of the model apartment.

"Navy brat, 'eh. Well that's good, that's real good. Say, I can't wait to get a look-see at this place." Dobs stepped in front of her and walked into the apartment first, exclaiming, "nice," as he did so, "real nice."

"This is the one bedroom and it is $600 a month. We have a two bedroom that is $850, if you need the extra room?"

"No, one bedroom is all I need, if you know what I mean." Smiling, he continued, "And this little area over here under the window," he began, indicating the dining area, "this is where the next award for screenwriter will be born, that you can be sure of!" His lack of modesty was compelling to Julie. He actually believed what he was saying.

"Write in a good part for me while you're at it," she exclaimed.

"Oh, I will. I will," he replied as he continued to look around the room. He looked back at her and said while smiling, "I'll take it."

After completing the paperwork at the office, Dobs drove his car around the parking lot until he found a place as close as possible to his new apartment. Everything he owned was in his trunk and his backseat and he wanted to unpack it all.

He had one suitcase with all of his clothes and a few boxes. The rest of the stuff in the trunk consisted of pictures to hang on the wall, a few movie posters (*Casablanca* and *Last Tango in Paris*), a couple of large pillows and two blankets, a portable cassette deck for sounds, and a bottle of J&B Scotch.

Once he had unloaded everything Dobs headed for the closest mattress store, which was on Wilshire. He was back in an hour with a promise that his new bed would be delivered by seven o'clock. He poured himself a scotch and water and sat down on one of his pillows, leaning it against the wall for support, and put on an Elton John tape to listen to while waiting for the delivery truck.

He loved this *Captain Fantastic and the Brown Dirt Cowboy* tape. His favorite song was "Someone Saved my Life Tonight" because it reminded him of Nikki up in San Francisco. He had met her one afternoon while hitting tennis balls by himself, volleying against himself against a tall cement wall that ran up behind the courts. He hadn't noticed her at first until he saw another ball hit the wall and bounce off back to his right. He turned and saw her and that was it. She was dark haired with olive colored skin and beautiful dark brown eyes. And when she asked him if he wanted to play a game he could only shake his head and say, "You bet I do."

He stared dumbly at her as they introduced each other and after a short time of volleying the tennis ball back and forth, she suggested that they go somewhere and get a drink. They ended up back at her place listening to Captain Fantastic, drinking slow sips of some kind of banana liquor, and smoking some hash in a small gold pipe before they ended up in her bedroom for the night. She played Joan Baez and Joni Mitchell songs on her guitar to him over a cup of hot tea and toast the next morning.

They were together all the time for about a month, slowly falling in love with each other, until her cousin Bradley came to visit from New York City and ended it all with his incessant nagging about Dobs not being Jewish and how upset her family back East would be that she was seeing him. She broke Dobs' heart when she told him she couldn't see him anymore, but it turned out for the best because it gave him a reason to leave town and head back to LA, which is where he was the most comfortable anyway. And, after all, his access to the industry was much greater in Los Angeles.

He dozed off on one of the big cushions and was awakened by the sound of the delivery guys knocking on his door at seven o'clock. In less than ten minutes his apartment actually looked like home. His new bed was made and his suitcase had been emptied, mostly on to a shelf in his closet. He had then taken a colorful beach towel and covered a cardboard box with it next to his bed to serve as a bedside table. He had covered his suitcase with another towel and set it up against the wall below the window and set the cassette deck on top of it. This would now serve as his entertainment center. There was room next to it for a small TV which he would buy the next day. He set a small black typewriter case that held his Royal portable typewriter at the foot of his bed. For now, this was home.

He poured himself another drink, changed into his swimsuit, and headed out for the hot tub he had noticed earlier not far from his unit. Once inside the hot bubbling water of the spa, he set his drink down on the concrete next to him and closed his eyes to relish the pleasure his tired and aching body was receiving from the jets in the water all around him. The water seemed to burn his skin somewhat but it still felt great. He was by himself for a few minutes before he heard Julie's voice over the sound of the spa bubbles.

"Make way for me!" She announced as she slid into the water across from him, her glistening body looking much better than he had initially thought it might when he had first met her.

"Closing time?" He asked, rubbing his eyes with his wet knuckles.

"Actually I closed at six. Just finished my workout and thought I would relax a bit. Oh, and by the way, don't get the water in your eyes. We just had it treated today. Some of the residents had complained about it so they did a full shock treatment on it earlier."

"Seems good to me," Dobs responded, now rubbing his eyes with the lower palms of his hands, "but it does kind of sting a bit."

"Probably killing all the germs!" Julie offered.

"Yeah, probably. Say, you have an agent, right?" he asked.

"Of course I do," she answered. "Not that its doing me much good," she complained, pouting.

"When did you work last?" He asked her.

"Been too long," she replied. "But I still expect a call any day."

"Yeah, sure you do." He paused before continuing. "I can write in a part for you if you like."

"You are on a project already?"

"Always," he answered her. "I have a script idea for Nicholson and I am fine tuning it as we speak."

"Yeah? And you have the contacts for that?" She inquired.

"You bet. I have someone who is going to get the treatment to him through Warren."

"Beatty?" she asked.

"Yeah, a friend of mine up north knows his sister and it's already a done deal." His confidence was not the least bit measured. "My friend grew up with Shirley and she will get it to Warren. Once he sees it, he'll realize it's perfect for Jack and then I will get the call. So I do have time to write in something for you, if you want?" Although this line had been used around Hollywood for many years, it still worked.

"Okay, do it. Then let me read it." She climbed out of the spa and dried herself off. Her skin wasn't quite as glistening to Dobs. In fact, everything looked fuzzy as he too decided to get out and head back to his place.

"I'll have it for you tomorrow," he said as he toweled off. "You working in the office tomorrow?"

"Yeah, ten to six," she answered him.

"I'll bring it by for you to check out after lunch."

"You can do it that fast?" She sounded surprised.

"Sure, it'll just be a small part. Won't take long." Rubbing his eyes he said goodnight and began walking back to his place. He took a shower and tried to wash off the hot tub water as best as he could before he poured himself a glass of ice water and went to bed.

When he woke up in the morning everything was black. He couldn't see anything at all. His eyes were sealed shut with a crusty glue-like substance. He tried to pry one eye open and it stung so bad he left it alone. Stumbling over to the sink he ran the water until it was warm and slowly began to gently massage his eyes with warm water until he could get them to crack open just a little, enough for him to see something. Enough for him to see how red and swollen his eyes were in the mirror! "What the fuck?" he said out loud.

He walked over to his closet and got dressed, feeling like his eyes were starting to seal shut again. He had to get to a telephone and he remembered seeing a payphone near the soda machine at the hot tub area last night. After getting dressed he headed out the door and made it to the payphone. He knew there was no way he could drive like this so he dialed information and asked for the number for Yellow Cab. He was told by the dispatcher that his cab would be there in ten minutes, and it was.

He squinted towards the entrance of the complex until he saw the taxi pull in and then he waved his arms until the driver saw him. Once inside, he could barely make out the features of the driver, a black woman in her twenties. He pulled out a twenty and handed it to her, saying, "Please, you've got to get me to the closest doctor's office and I can't see to read the phone book. But you know some place, right?" Assuming correctly that she knew exactly where the closest doctor's office was.

She took his twenty and told him not to worry about it. Just sit back and relax. Within five minutes she pulled into a medical center's parking lot and said, "Here you go, right up there in front of the place is a family practice that can probably help you. How in the world did you get both eyes so messed up anyways? You look like you been stung in both eyes by some kind of insect!" She parked the cab and got out to help Dobs out and to walk him up the path to the office entrance.

Feeling helpless, Dobs asked her, "Anyway you could come back and get me when I am through here?" He pulled another twenty out of his pants pocket and handed it to her. She refused to take it and said you just have them call Yellow Cab and ask for number 199 and I'll come back and pick you up, you keep this twenty."

"What's your name, 199?" Dobs asked, squinting to see her.

"Gladys," she answered. "But ask for 199, not Gladys."

"Will do - and I really, really appreciate your help!" He smiled at her and turned to enter the office.

Without an appointment he had to wait for almost two hours before anyone could see him, but he could tell the front desk girl really felt bad for him and he was just grateful to get in and get some drops for his eyes. The doctor told him it would take a few days to clear up so he was stuck at home for a while. He asked the girl at the front desk to call his taxi back for him and ask for 199. In about fifteen minutes he saw Gladys walk in the front door and he got up to leave.

"So," she said to him as he walked down the sidewalk towards the cab, "things lookin' better for you?"

"Not until we get my drops," he answered. "I bet there is a pharmacy close to here, right?"

"Right across the street," she said as they both got into the cab. They crossed the street and got the drops and were soon back at Dobs' apartment complex.

"Gladys, I can't thank you enough. How much do I owe you?" he asked.

"Well, let's see, you paid me twenty earlier and we only went about five miles altogether so I would say we are good."

"Really, that's awfully sweet of you. You're sure about that now?" he asked.

"I'm sure, unless you want to invite me over sometime for a hot tub," she said as she looked over at the spa area.

"You don't want to get into that thing. Look what it did to me!" he exclaimed as he pointed to his still swollen eyes. "But, give me your number and when I am better I will give you a call and buy you a drink."

"You got it," she said as she wrote her number on a piece of paper. "I am a hack three days a week with this cab and I also work at the Warner Brothers lot doing some security work, so I'm pretty busy. But do give me a call when you are feeling better." She handed him the piece of paper and got back into her cab as she said, "So long for now."

Dobs' vision was a little better after taking the drops and he was just realizing how attractive Gladys really was, saying, "I'll call you," as she said goodbye.

He turned and began walking towards his apartment and remembered his promise to Julie about the script he would include her in. "Oh well," he thought to himself, "that won't be happening today." Once inside, he climbed into bed with a warm wash cloth over his eyes and began to mentally work out the details of Julie's minor role in his story.

He was sound asleep by the time Julie knocked on his door after she had closed the leasing office at six o'clock. His eyelids were stuck together again and he had to wet the wash cloth with warm water and rub some of the crustiness away before answering the door, looking like a freak. "Sorry it took a while, come in."

"What the hell happened to you?" Julie asked.

"Your hot tub, I guess. Double shot of conjunctivitis for me." He moved back over to his bed.

"So I guess you are out of it for a few days?" she replied.

"Looks like it, doesn't it!" He laughed at his joke before continuing. "I'll get your part done by the end of the week. No rush, right?"

"No, not at all. But I do hope you're better by Friday night. My friend, Starlie, from England, she got me an extra ticket to the Whiskey on Friday night. Know who's gonna be there, upstairs?" She was referring to a private club above the Whiskey a Go-Go on Sunset, a club frequented by rock stars and other celebs. "*Led Zeppelin,* after they finish their concert, they are coming by the club. She writes for the *NME* and has an interview with them, and we get to meet them."

"What's the *NME*?" Dobs asked.

"England's version of *Rolling Stone Magazine*," she answered.

"Oh, I see," he said as he removed the washcloth, smiling, "not really!" He was trying to be funny again.

"Anyway, I thought I could let you tag along since you are doing a favor for me with the script."

He had been a *Led Zeppelin* fan back in the late 60's but hadn't paid much attention to their early 70s work. "Sounds good I guess, if I can see by then that is!"

Julie walked over and sat down on the edge of his bed. "Can I get you something, Dobs?"

"I am hungry. Could you order me a pizza, maybe?" he asked.

"Absolutely," she answered, "with what toppings? Pepperoni and mushroom, okay?"

"Sure, that's great and a coke too, maybe. I really appreciate it. The doctor said I should be a lot better by tomorrow." He reached into his pocket and gave her some money, saying, "I insist."

Julie left and he put on an old Zeppelin tape he had in his collection, the one with *Whole Lot of Love* on it. He drifted off again while he was listening to it. When Julie returned they ate the pizza together, listened to a little music, and then she said goodnight.

The next morning his eyes were better. Not good enough to drive yet but maybe good enough to see the typewriter keys. He began working on the script and by noon Julie's part was integrated into a scene where Jack Nicholson, in an irate mood, is trying to check into a hotel room and they are telling him that they have no rooms left, even though he had made a reservation. Julie would be the adorable young lady standing behind Jack as he calmly argued with the desk clerk about his room. Julie would be the one to offer him an extra room she had reserved but no longer needed. It allowed for enough dialog to give Julie a decent appearance and, after all, it would be a scene with Jack.

By Friday night his eyesight was back to 100% and when he first saw Robert Plant enter the club, on crutches no less, he was surprised at how short he was. Apparently he had just been in a terrible auto accident and was nursing along a break or two. But he had just performed at the Bowl and had probably done so without the crutches. Julie and her friend Starlie were about as lit up as they could be about meeting Plant and his band, but to Dobs, it really wasn't that big of a deal.

But when Starlie told him later that night that she had a close friend who was working on a new Cassavetes film project, and that they would all be meeting out at Martin Sheen's home in Malibu on Sunday afternoon to discuss it, and that they had asked her if she knew of a good dialog coach, Dobs was all over it.

The Sunday drive down Sunset to Malibu with Julie and Starlie was about as good as it gets, as far as Dobs was concerned. He already had it mapped out in his head about how he was now on the same level as the young Orson Wells had been when working on multiple projects. Between his Nicholson film and this John Cassavetes project he would soon be a part of, wow, he was stoked.

The Sheens lived in a modest – for Malibu – ranch home that could have been a house in any affluent neighborhood in America. The two boys, Charlie and Emilio, had left their bikes out in the front yard, thoughtlessly thrown down on to the lawn before running off to find another game to play while Dad had his business meeting. Mrs. Sheen was elegant, both in appearance and manner, as she greeted everyone at the front door.

Dobs had parked the yellow Camaro up on the street near the entrance to the driveway behind a few other cars that were lining the road. He walked down the driveway, then to the front of the house to be greeted by Mrs. Sheen who was standing at the front door.

Once inside, he saw Martin Sheen (who was, surprisingly, as short as Robert Plant had been) standing in the living room and Dobs approached him immediately. He introduced himself as a writer and possible dialog coach for the project and then, seeing a small room or study off to the side of the living room, and noticing the wall was adorned with plaques and awards, he motioned for Martin to take him into the room.

The walls were covered with awards and posters from past theatre work Sheen had been in and he was very proud of them as he began reminiscing to Dobs about the good old days. Once he got going, and with the help of Dobs' own sincere enthusiasm, they spent the next ten minutes or so talking about Sheen's early days in theatre. When they heard the meeting in the living room start to begin, they both left the study feeling somewhat comfortable with each other; Dobs felt like he was running with an equal and Sheen was just happy to have someone to share his experiences with.

Dobs had intentionally not mentioned his Nicholson screenplay to Martin Sheen. When he heard that this Cassavetes project involved all of them going to Colorado to shoot the entire film in a barn, he knew it wasn't for him. But he also knew he should keep this budding new relationship going with Sheen, so he did not let it be known that he had no interest in the project.

After an hour or so they all took a break and he excused himself, said goodbye to Sheen, and gathered up Starlie and Julie, telling them he had to leave. Starlie, who wanted to be discovered, fought him on it; Julie was fine with it.

The following week Starlie called Julie and told her she had a part in the project and was on her way to Colorado with the crew. Julie came over to Dobs' place and let him know what had happened. She was surprised when he told her he had decided to pass on the Cassavetes film because of his own project. "Are you sure about that?" she asked him.

"Yeah, don't need it. Don't have the time for it." Little did he know then that he would relive this moment for years and years as the moment when he could have chosen a different path. It actually woke him up now as he recalled it.

He had blown it. His screenplay never got close to Nicholson and his money had run out by the end of the year. He took a job as an inside sales rep for an investment firm in Westwood.

As he sat in his recliner and rubbed his eyes, he told himself that his young dreams had been foolish and that he was much better off today as a financial adviser than he would have ever been as a successful screenwriter. And it was only a faint little voice inside of him that laughed and told him he was wrong.

CHAPTER 2

Now, here he was in the summer of 2010 applying for a job at Charles Schwab in Anaheim. As he walked down the sidewalk on Katella Avenue he could see the entrance to Disneyland a few blocks ahead. The Charles Schwab office was on his right just a few doors ahead.

Walking into the lobby he was greeted by an attractive young woman in her early twenties. He told her he was there to see a Mr. Morgan for an interview and took a seat on one of the nicely cushioned chairs in the reception area. A flat screen TV was broadcasting CNBC and he saw that the Dow Jones Index was down about 300 points. He had grown to loathe this business but it was all he had ever done. Now that he had moved to Orange County from LA he needed a job that was close, and most of his client base wanted discounted commissions. Schwab was the perfect choice. And the fact that it was so close to Disney and all the nice hotels and restaurants nearby was a plus. Many of his clients could now fly in with their families, meet with him to discuss their portfolio, enjoy a few days in the OC, and fly back home with a nice tax deductible expense.

Mr. Morgan offered him the job and he accepted it. His client base and his thirty plus years of experience would be a great asset to this Schwab office, he was told by Steve Morgan, his new boss, who was about twenty years younger than Dobs. He was told he could start as soon his Series 7 license transfer took place, maybe a day or two.

He was given a brief tour of the office and Mr. Morgan showed him where his desk would be. Shaking hands and thanking him, Dobs left the office and walked back out on to Katella Avenue.

Once back in his car he headed back towards Huntington Beach and the new condo he had just bought. He had sold his home in Thousand Oaks, where he had lived for years, for a nice profit. He was able to buy a 1500 square foot condo in Huntington Beach for $529,000 and it was only a few blocks from the ocean in the downtown area, near Main Street. He had thought about buying a single family home but decided against it since he was now by himself. A condo was all he needed.

He had been married for twenty years to a great lady but she had left him for a younger man the year before. He knew when he married her that because she was twelve years younger it might be a problem one day, and that's how it had played out. She had met a guy at her office and after a short affair she told Dobs that she still really loved him but wanted to be with the other guy. His only child, Dawn, was in her second year at UCLA and lived with her boyfriend in Westwood. So, according to his wife, the transition would be easy. After a six month period of depression and too much alcohol, Dobs had pulled himself together enough to sell the house, split the proceeds with his ex-wife, and move to Huntington Beach.

Dobs had been somewhat reluctant to move to Orange County, having spent most of his life in Los Angeles. OC was a different kind of place than LA. The people were different, the culture was different. Even the air was different - a lot cleaner. And the ocean seemed to bring a calm to the place that did not exist in the coastal areas north of Seal Beach. The air seemed to not only be dirtier the farther north one traveled on PCH, but it also seemed to get a lot more "tense" with the ambient anxiety of the greater Los Angeles area. Orange County was a more relaxing place to live, or so Dobs felt when he decided to make the move. And he needed a little relaxation in his life right now.

He drove into Huntington Beach and arrived at his condo about four o'clock. He had no plans for the evening yet he felt the need to celebrate his new job at Schwab. He called his daughter and let her know about it. He had always been very close to her. When she left home to move into an apartment near the campus his life had become half-empty. If he had not had marital problems it might have approached half-full, but with his wife already talking about divorce it was definitely half-empty.

Dawn answered her cell quickly and Dobs told her about the job and asked her if she could come down to have dinner with him on Sunday night. She said she would take him out to dinner tonight to celebrate and she would be at his new place by seven o'clock.

As he disconnected the call he smiled, so happy to have her for a daughter. He would take her to Olive Garden for dinner. It was one of her favorite places and had been all her life. They had taken her there every birthday since she was little.

Pulling into his reserved parking space at his complex, he looked out the passenger side window at the late afternoon sun that was just beginning its descent into the Pacific, staying hidden behind spectacular orange cloud formations as it moved towards the ocean.

As he sat in his car and relaxed, the quiet was quickly interrupted by a loud thumping bass sound that emanated from a car that had just driven slowly by the entrance of his complex. His first thought was that he had left all of that crap behind him in LA, but realizing the absurdity of that notion he shook his head and got out of the car. He stood gazing at the slow moving silver Humvee from where the sound originated as it turned the corner on to 6th Street.

As he walked into the open atrium area that was surrounded by lush plants and trees he felt very good about his new home. He walked up to the ground floor entrance of his condo and pulled a flyer off the front door that offered a menu and a coupon for a new barbeque place on

Main Street. He brought it inside and put it on to the door of his new stainless steel Maytag refrigerator he had just purchased the week before. Then he opened up the fridge and grabbed a cold Corona. Sitting out on his deck, which not only gave him a partial view of the Pacific but a good section of the atrium's garden as well, he contemplated his new life while he waited for Dawn to arrive.

As it occasionally did, his thoughts turned to writing a screenplay again. Of the several great ideas he had come up with over the years, no one else had yet produced anything the least bit similar. This gave him some hope and encouragement, although it was not enough to motivate him to begin writing. He enjoyed just thinking it all through and occasionally sharing his ideas with whoever would listen. He dozed off and was awakened by Dawn's arrival at seven o'clock, rubbing his eyes as he answered the door.

"Hi Dad!" She gave him a big hug. "Congratz on the job. So you going to become a surfer dude here in Huntington?" She loved to tease him.

"Yeah, right. That's me." Closing the door, he said, "Olive Garden?"

"Well, how about something different. Maybe Harpoon Harry's? Didn't you and Mom used to love going there?" Dawn was surprising him.

"Yeah, and we even took you there a few times too. They have great Shrimp Scampi. Let's do it." Dobs sounded excited enough about it as he grabbed his car keys off the kitchen counter.

Dobs and his daughter headed out of the complex and turned on to 6th Street heading down towards PCH. Dawn spoke first, "Dad, I need to tell you something."

"Let's hear it."

"Tim asked me to marry him and I said yes." She sounded very happy.

"That's great, hon. But shouldn't you wait a while and finish at UCLA?"

"Well, that's just it. Tim signed up with the Marines yesterday and he goes for boot camp next month in San Diego. Hopefully he gets stationed there after his training and I can continue at UC San Diego." She sounded nervous.

"Or wherever else they might station him! Hawaii maybe? Or, God forbid, 29 Palms out in the Mohave Desert." Dobs was trying to be supportive but his mind was starting to race about the future. He now stood to lose his daughter too.

"But if they do Camp Pendleton I will still be close to you, right? I think it's only an hour away."

"Let's hope that's what happens!" Dobs said before adding, "Well, Congratulations sweetie!"

"Thanks Dad. Tim wants to formally ask your permission."

"Tell him he's got it." Dobs responded before driving in silence for a few minutes down the Pacific Coast Highway towards Sunset Beach.

Dawn broke the silence. "He wanted to come tonight and ask you but I said I wanted to be with you alone to tell you about it."

"Thanks, sweetie. I can see him this weekend. Tonight can just be father and daughter night!" Dobs was growing somewhat melancholic as he pulled into the restaurant, realizing that his life was changing even quicker than he had thought possible.

The next morning he really began to fret about possibly losing his relationship with his daughter. If they sent them overseas, or too far away, he would not see her anymore - except on those rare occasions when they came home for leave. He wanted to call his ex-wife and talk to her about it but decided against it.

He had the day to kill while he waited on his license transfer to Schwab so he decided to log on to Facebook. Dawn had talked a lot about it at dinner the night before, how she and her friends stayed connected that way. If she was going to be leaving the area, this might be something he should spend some time with. He had established an account last year but never really used it that much.

When he logged on he saw a friend request that blew him away. It was a request from Nikki Pitilon. It was a request from Nikki. San Francisco Nikki - from 1975. Dobs sat there staring at the screen in a semi-stupor. How could it be? She had remembered his name. She had contacted him!

His hand almost trembled when he clicked on the link to accept her as a friend. Then it occurred to him that she would be looking at his profile soon. It needed work, to say the least. He spent the next hour adding a few good photos of himself, enhancing his "likes and interests" to include a few new films he liked and, just for old times sake, he added Elton John. When he was through he was pleased with the new result and knew she would contact him. Once she accepted him as a friend he could view her private profile. Maybe she had a photo of herself posted. He could only imagine.

At this point Dobs decided that his life was actually spinning out of control to some degree. Too much was happening, too fast. He stared at the monitor and remembered the time he had spent in San Francisco with Nikki. So, quickly doing the math, she must be about fifty-five years old now – about his age.

As he sat there thinking about her his eye caught a small Facebook advertisement about foster children. That's something he could look into, he thought to himself while he waited for a reply from Nikki. He knew it might be days before she checked her account again but that didn't stop him from staring at the screen and daydreaming about becoming a foster parent to some poor kid who had nothing going for himself, or herself. The ad had a photo of some smiling teenagers and a 310 area code phone number. So it was a local agency placing the ad. He decided to call them while he waited for Nikki's response.

His mind was not completely on what he was saying to the agency as it drifted back to his days with Nikki while he spoke to a counselor. Before he fully realized what he had done, he was giving his home address to the agency and had scheduled an appointment for someone to come see him the following Monday morning. He was thanking the counselor when he saw a blink on his computer and realized that Nikki had just responded.

He opened up her profile and stared at her photo. She looked about thirty-five and was gorgeous. She lived in Laguna Beach. Not quite ten minutes away from Huntington Beach. Dobs felt like he was going to have diarrhea at this point from all the excitement.

How could that be? So close. And she had contacted him. After a few minutes in the bathroom Dobs felt a lot better. After all, they were both adults and he would just ask her out to dinner to talk about old times. No big deal, right?

He sent her an email with his number and asked her if he could buy her dinner in Laguna at Las Brisas sometime this weekend, whatever worked for her. Within a few minutes she answered back and a time and date were set for Sunday at noon for brunch.

The next few days were an eternity for Dobs as he waited for Sunday morning to roll around. When it did, he was up at seven o'clock. He decided on a Hawaiian shirt with royal blue flowers on it and khaki shorts. He had gone to a hair salon the day before and he was pleased with the look they gave his hair. Actually, he felt very confident as he got into his car and headed for Laguna Beach an hour before he even needed to be there. He would spend the time walking along the beach, soaking up some sun.

At noon he was stationed by the front door of Las Brisas, and when Nikki arrived she looked so good that he was almost speechless. He had reserved a table outside and as they began to make small talk he realized he was still crazy about her. He only hoped that she felt the same way. She wore a straw sun hat with a colorful scarf tied around it that nearly matched his shirt. "Too much!" he thought to himself.

"So Dobs, you are a successful money manager?" Nikki said.

"Yes, I suppose. Hardly the successful screenwriter I planned on being when I first met you." Dobs replied. "How about you? What did you end up doing?"

"I run a fitness studio in Corona del Mar. And I have two daughters - but I never married," she offered. "I adopted both of my girls last year."

"Really? How old are they?" Dobbs sounded surprised.

"Thirteen and fifteen. But they are not related to each other. They were both in the system together and were best friends. Because I was successful and could control my working hours they let me take them as a foster mom two years ago. Last year the adoption was official." Nikki was obviously very proud of what she had done.

"You know, I have an appointment on Monday to meet with someone from an agency in LA about the same thing. Maybe I should take on two boys about the same age as your girls! What a trip that would be." He felt foolish as soon as he had said it.

"It's a lot of work but it's worth it." Nikki took a sip from her champagne glass.

"And how do you manage to look so good? You look twenty years younger than me," Dobs said, changing the subject.

"That's my job." Nikki answered. "Remember? Fitness?"

"Of course." He stared over her shoulder to the white sand below and the ocean beyond it. The waves were only a few feet high and the sound of them breaking was audible in the distance. He looked back at her and couldn't imagine that she would have any more interest in him but, surprisingly, she seemed to be showing just that.

"But you have a daughter, correct?" She had carefully read his Facebook profile.

"Yeah, Dawn. She is getting married to a Marine soon and will be shipping out with him to wherever he is stationed."

"You don't sound very happy about that?" Nikki pried.

"No, I'm not. She and I have always been very close."

"And that is why you are thinking about foster parenting now?"

"I suppose."

"Well you better be ready for anything," Nikki told him, adding, "You know, my daughters have told me some stories. Some of the places they lived were horrible, so the kids grow up real tough."

"That's what I figured. I think I can handle it, but my job will probably stand in the way. I am at the office from seven to four each day. They probably won't like that."

"They told me the only way they could let me have my girls was if I could be at home for them whenever they needed me. My studio is just down the block from my house, so it worked out well for me. You might have a problem, though." Nikki sounded pretty sure about this.

"Well, if they say no, they say no. At least I tried." After they finished their breakfast, Dobs suggested,

"How about a walk through town. Maybe show me your studio?" Dobs was sure she would agree to this.

"I'm sorry. I have to go the movies with my girls at two." She paused for a moment. "But why not come for dinner?"

"Really?" He thought he sounded like an idiot. "I'd love to."

She wrote down her address and phone number and handed it to him. "About seven o'clock?"

"Definitely," he said as he stood up and stared at her. "I still can't believe you found me on Facebook. And how great you look."

"Well, I sent out requests to anyone I had ever had some kind of meaningful relationship with and you were on the list."

"There's a list?" he asked, sounding somewhat insecure.

"Yes, a few men I have known. But you are the only one I have found so far."

"And I am so glad I made it on to your list." Dobs pulled her chair out and they walked out of the restaurant together. He walked her down the sidewalk towards her house for a block or two before he said goodbye until later.

"See you at seven." She stood there in the sun looking ravishing. How could she look so good at her age? Dobs stared in amazement, knowing he would have to work very hard to make this go anywhere.

He called Dawn on his way back to the car and told her he had met someone. Through Facebook. Thanks to her talking about it so much last night. Unbelievable.

What were the chances? And to have happened as soon as he logged in. It was definitely a meant to be situation. He kept rambling on like that and Dawn listened, happy that her father was so excited about something.

Late that afternoon, after going home to shower and change, he arrived at the address Nikki had given him. He knocked on the door and it was opened by a man that could only be described as huge – Schwarzenegger in his prime huge. He was about thirty and had no shirt on. His oiled skin glistened in the late afternoon sun. "What the fuck?" Dobs thought to himself before saying, "Hi there. Is Nikki here?"

"Sure, he said, with no Austrian accent, come on in. I was just leaving. I am Paul, one of her trainers. Come on in. She is upstairs getting dressed."

Dobs entered the living room, totally confused. He watched as Paul gathered up his things, put them in a small black satchel, and left. Standing alone in the living room he looked around and saw quite a few awards that Nikki must have won. He got closer and saw that they were actually awards for dancing, and they were not Nikki's. They belonged to someone named Allison.

As he was looking at one of the small trophies he heard someone quietly walk up behind him. "Hello," a female voice said. "I'm Allison, and this is my sister, Jamie." He turned around and saw two teenage girls standing in the living room, one a little older than the other.

"Hello there Allison. And Jamie. So Allison, these awards, very impressive." Dobs wanted to win them both over quickly.

"Oh, it was nothing. I'm just a good dancer in a class with a bunch of girls who can't dance very well. They mostly live in Corona and Newport and their parents have mega bucks to spend on dance classes for them. Really, it's embarrassing. I always seem to win the awards. I actually love singing a lot more than dancing. I just love Stevie Niks in Fleetwood Mac!" Allison was blond and must have been the 15 year old. Next to her was Jamie, maybe thirteen years old he guessed.

"And Jamie, are you a dancer too?" he asked.

"Not really. That's her department," she answered. "I'm mostly into hip-hop."

The smell of a simmering marinara was permeating the entire house and it smelled wonderful. "Smells good. What did she make?"

"Lasagna," answered Jamie. "And it's really good, too."

"I'm sure it is. Where is she anyway?" Dobs turned to walk towards the kitchen, beginning to feel somewhat awkward just as Nikki came down the stairs. She was wearing a bright yellow tank top and blue jean shorts. Her dark brown hair was tied in a bun on top of her head. She smiled at Dobs as she said, "So you have met the girls I see."

"Yeah. I'm impressed. Allison says she loves Fleetwood Mac. And that was so long ago."

"Yes, but just think about all the different homes she's been in. It must have had quite an impression on her somewhere along the line."

"And I met Paul too," he added. "Quite a physique on the man."

"He is in great shape. He runs the studio for me when I need him to." Nikki walked over to him and kissed him on the cheek. "Hungry?"

"You bet!" he said as he followed her into the kitchen. "So does Paul stay here with you?"

"No, he lives in Costa Mesa. He drops by on his way home a lot, just to check on me." Nikki was stirring the sauce.

"Looks like he would be a great protector. Hope I don't do anything to upset the man."

Nikki was taking the cork out of a bottle of Chianti. "Glass of wine?" she asked.

"Sure." She moved towards him and reached up to get two glasses from a rack that was mounted below the upper kitchen cabinet. "I hope you like the dinner."

"I'm sure I will," he said as he got a nice close shot of her breasts as she reached for the glasses. No way she looked that good, he thought to himself.

At dinner she told him about the hassles she had gone through trying to adopt the girls. She also told him about her passion for fitness. He knew he was in terrible shape physically. He could probably run a mile if he had to, that was it. He played tennis once or twice a month and occasionally played a round of golf, but that was it. How would she ever have any interest in him? Oh well, it was great to see her, he thought to himself as he finished his dinner and looked across the table at her beautiful face.

"So," she began, after the girls had cleared the table, "you want to sleepover?"

He sat stunned and speechless for a moment before responding. "Of course I do." He still wasn't sure if she meant for him to sleep on the sofa or sleep with her.

She stood up and walked over to his end of the table and put her arms around him as she pulled his head to nestle in her breasts, saying to him, "It's been so, so, long."

Dobs face was buried against her firm chest as he tried to reply but decided against it. Hearing the girls coming back into the room, Nikki quickly broke away from Dobs and began asking them to serve the apple pie she had made.

After the table had been cleared and the girls had retired to their bedroom upstairs, Nikki asked Dobs to join her for a walk along the beach. Crossing over PCH, which was still very busy with traffic at nine o'clock, they walked silently towards the ocean.

As they walked along the shoreline together, Nikki told Dobs why she had tried to contact him. She told him that she had looked back on her life to the very best of times and decided that she would try to reconnect. He had been her first choice and she was so happy she had found him.

"But your life seems so good?" Dobs responded. "You've got the girls, and the house, and the great business?"

Nikki stopped walking and put her arms around his shoulders with her face just inches from his. "But I don't have a great man in my life," she said before she kissed him. "And you, from what I remember, were very great!" She laughed and kissed him again.

Dobs pretty much melted into her arms. The first time he had been with a woman in months, and the first time he had been with someone he really liked in years. They both turned together in the sand as they headed back up towards PCH and her place.

They had only been gone about an hour but when they turned on to her street they saw the police cars in front of her house, red and blue lights still flashing on one of the cars. As they ran closer they saw that a blond haired woman was in the back seat of one of the cars.

"That crazy bitch!" exclaimed Nikki as they approached the closest officer. "I live here. Are my daughters okay?"

"They are fine ma'am. We got a call and picked this one up," he said, motioning to the woman in the backseat of his car, "after your daughter called us. She was pounding on the front door and scared them half to death. So you know her, ma'am?"

"She's a lunatic that keeps trying to see my girls. I adopted them last year and she claims she is the biological mother of the older one." Nikki spoke calmly to the officer as Dobs took it all in.

"So she has bothered you before? Is she really the girl's mother?" the officer asked.

"I don't know. The first time I saw her was last week. I woke up in the morning and she was doing some kind of ballet exercise on my front lawn at six thirty. I asked her what she was doing and she ran off. She was back the next day trying to take a picture of the girls as we left for school. She approached me and informed me that she was Allison's birth mother and was here to take her back. I called the police and they came and got her. Now this."

"And that's the only contact you have had with her?"

"Yes sir." Nikki gave Dobs a troubled look as she said to him, "I am so sorry to drag you into all of this." Then she turned to the officer and said, "I think you should probably have her examined. I don't think she is all there, if you know what I mean."

"I think you are right ma'am," he responded, adding, "and you too have a good night." He turned and got back into his car as the other car drove away.

"That was weird," Dobs announced.

"Yeah, weird." Nikki agreed as they both walked up to the house to calm the girls.

Dobs did spend the night that night but there was not much sleeping. Nikki wore him out in the first two hours and they spent the rest of the night sharing stories with each other about what they had been up to for the last few decades.

The next morning Dobs offered to have an attorney friend of his call her to possibly help her out with the birth mom lady. Maybe get a restraining order. Nikki thanked him as she kissed him goodbye and left to drop the girls off at school. Dobs took his time getting ready to leave, making himself another cup of coffee and sitting on her porch for a few minutes before leaving. It wasn't until he was on the PCH headed back towards Huntington that he remembered his appointment this morning with the counselor.

As he drove home he thought back to some of the things Nikki had told him the night before. She had lived with the same man for fifteen years before finally developing the courage to leave him after one too many beatings. He would reach a point after drinking more than four or five beers when he would become a different person. His face would even change. His eyes would grow dark. And he would beat her senseless, sometimes even holding a knife to her neck. But when he came out of it, he would cry and apologize so profusely that she would be reluctant to report him. She actually loved this side of his psychosis so much that she would put up with the abuse. Until finally she had taken enough and called the police. He was still serving time in prison and would not be up for parole for three more years.

Dobs decided that if the guy ever got out and approached Nikki he would spend whatever was necessary to have him eliminated from her life permanently. No one deserved that kind of treatment, but especially not his Nikki. His Nikki. He laughed out loud, before exclaiming to himself, "Unfucking believable!"

As he turned into his complex he decided to call the agency and see if he could cancel his appointment. Once inside he dialed the number and yes, he had been able to reach them in time. They would contact the counselor and cancel for him. After that was done he showered and got into bed for a nap, something he never did, but why not? He deserved it. As he dozed off to sleep he pictured a new life together with Nikki and the two girls and fell asleep happy. He was awakened an hour later by a phone call from Steve Morgan at Schwab, telling him his license transfer had gone through and that he could start his new job the next day.

CHAPTER 3

Andrea, or Andi, as she preferred to be called, sat in the back seat of the police car and stared out the window at the night sky as they traveled along the 55 towards Santa Ana, where the Orange County jail was located. She knew they were probably going to hold her overnight and then release her in the morning, just like last time. She wished she had brought her meds with her. But they would have probably taken them away again, just like the last time. She needed them for her bipolar disorder. It would come and go. As long as she took her meds daily she could ride out the rough times, but when she missed a day or two, everything got all screwed up. She would just take them when she got back to her house in the morning.

She knew she needed to stop getting arrested like this or she would never get her daughter back. Her precious angel, Allison, she had given up at birth fifteen years ago when that asshole Ron had gotten her pregnant. He had told her he was using a condom. Like a fool she had believed him.

When the deputy sheriff's car pulled into the jail facility and she was taken into the intake area, she began to feel a little woozy. Probably from stress, she told herself. Who wouldn't be stressed in a situation like this? She looked across the room at the clock on the wall. It was almost eleven o'clock. It would be a long night.

The next morning she was arraigned and charged with trespassing. Bail was set at $2,000 and she used her debit card to pay it. On her way home in a taxi, she focused on her plan to get her Alli back. It had taken her years to track her down, and when she had finally found her the adoption had just gone through. She hadn't even been allowed by the system to challenge it as the natural birth mother. The adoption had been final. If only she had found her earlier. But, after all, she hadn't really been looking for her that hard earlier.

Her career as an artist had taken priority over everything. She had developed quite a reputation as a wedding artist. She would travel the country to different weddings where she would paint a portrait of bride and groom, sometimes making as much as $5,000 in one afternoon. It only took her a few hours to do it and she was very good at it, as long as she took her meds on a daily basis. If she missed a few days there was no telling where she would end up.

CHAPTER 3

One weekend she ended up in Dallas, where she was supposed to do a painting on a Saturday but somehow ended up at a rodeo, where she attempted to convince one of the cowboys she was there to do a painting of him. Of course, having no idea what she was talking about, he ignored her. She then drove her rental car all the way to El Paso. Not sure why she was there, she turned around and drove back to Dallas, from where she somehow made it to the airport and then back to Orange County by Sunday night. Another weekend with no meds had passed.

As she had the taxi drop her off in front of her house in Lake Forest, she realized her car was still parked in Laguna Beach, close to Nikki's place. She knocked on the taxi's window and got back in to the cab, asking him to take her to Laguna for her car. As she thought about the night before, and how much she wanted her daughter back, she began to weep quietly. The driver noticed it and asked her if she was alright. She nodded her head yes and continued to cry all the way to Laguna Beach.

Once behind the wheel of her minivan again, she felt much better. She decided to drive by Alli's school and see if she could maybe see her walking across the campus. She parked the minivan in a spot close to the front of the school and waited patiently, watching the kids move from class to class. After about an hour and not seeing Alli, she decided to drive home and shower. Maybe come back after school to see if she needed a ride.

At home she reviewed her bottles of meds arranged neatly on the top of the island in the kitchen. She left them there so she would always remember to take them, not that it always worked. She was so excited about getting her daughter back she almost missed her lunchtime pills. But seeing the bottle now reminded her to take them. Bipolar was a bitch.

Once back in front of the school that afternoon, she sat in the minivan and listened to a Shania Twain CD while she waited for dismissal. Once the bell rang and the kids began pouring out of the building, she climbed out of the vehicle and began scanning the crowd for a sign of Allison.

Nikki was just pulling up in front of the school to pick up her daughter when she saw the crazy bitch standing there staring at the crowd of kids. She wanted to get out of her car and inflict some serious physical pain on her but thought the better of it and just parked her car across the street and called Allison's cell. When she answered she told her to walk around to the side of the school by the gym and she would pick her up there.

Nikki started her car and slowly pulled into the traffic to make a right up past the gym. She kept an eye on the crazy lady just to make sure she wasn't following her. She wasn't.

As Nikki pulled up to the entrance of the gym and Allison and Jamie got into he car, she said to them, "We have to have a talk." The girls gave each other a puzzled look as she continued. "You know that woman that came to the house the other night? The one the police took away. Well," Nikki paused and looked directly at Allison who was seated in the passenger seat next to her. "She claims she is your birth mother."

"What?" Allison exclaimed. "How could that be?"

"That's just it, Allison. It might not be. And even if it is she gave you up fifteen years ago and I am your mother now. She is trying to snatch you up and take you away from me. She was waiting for you in front of the school. That's why I had you walk around here to this side." Nikki pulled out into the traffic again and began to head for home as she continued. "And I have to do something about her. I'm supposed to see a lawyer later today. I have no idea what he will recommend but at least I can get some kind of protection order to keep her away from you for now."

"But she might be my real mother?" Allison offered nervously.

"Yeah, honey. A real Mom. Put you up for adoption as soon as you were born," Nikki explained as Allison looked at Jamie in the backseat. "But she does claim she gave you your name before she turned you in to child services."

Jamie spoke up first, saying, "So it might be her real mother? Right?"

"That's right. Or just a very bad person. Or maybe both, I don't know. I am taking you guys to the studio where Paul can keep an eye on you and I am driving into Santa Monica to meet with the attorney. Just keep an eye out for her and do not get near her. If you see her call me. I'll be back by dinnertime." Nikki looked at Jamie in the rear view window and then back at Allison as she said, "And you two girls know how much I love you, right?" Allison and Jamie nodded in agreement but said nothing.

Later that afternoon, on her way home from Santa Monica, Nikki called Dobs to thank him for the referral.

The lawyer had been very impressive, very helpful. He had told her he would have the restraining order issued within a few days and suggested she find some new place to stay with the girls until he was able to finalize it. He had suggested she ask Dobs for help.

"Of course I'll help you. You guys can stay here at my place for the next few days. I have an extra guest room for the girls." He was thrilled to get her call as he drove down the 405 towards home. "I'll be at work most of the day and you guys can just hang out and enjoy the change of scenery. I knew Max would be able to help you out," he said to her, referring to his attorney friend.

"Thank you so much, Dobs. I really appreciate it! And I owe you big time," Nikki responded. "That woman is psycho. Can you believe her? Coming to my house like that?"

"Yeah, I know." Dobs took the Warner Avenue exit as he continued speaking. "So you'll be over tonight, right?

"Guess so. I am heading back now to pick them up, and then I am taking you and the girls out to dinner. Got a good family place close to home?"

"Olive Garden. Right around the corner from me."

"Perfect. We'll be at your place about seven o'clock." She got the address from him and entered it into her GPS on the dash as she drove down Newport Boulevard towards home.

As she pulled into her driveway she saw the tan VW minivan parked in front of her house and Andrea standing in the driveway, arms crossed. She pulled into the driveway and jumped out of the car, walking quickly up to Andrea and staring into her crazed face. "You crazy fucking bitch. How dare you come back to this house? I will kick your ass into tomorrow, do you understand?"

Andrea was unmoved as she said, "I just want my daughter back. That's all. Is that really asking too much?"

"Asking too much?" Nikki shouted. "She is not your daughter, never has been. You gave her up, correct? I adopted her. Now get the fuck off of my property." Nikki dialed 911 on her cell phone.

"Calling the police again? How pathetic. You can not even stand to simply talk through this like a mature adult. I can't believe they gave you custody of anyone."

Nikki held the small flip phone tightly in her right fist as she pulled it back and launched a ferocious blow on to Andrea's chin that quickly knocked her to the ground and almost into unconsciousness. "Now get the hell off of my property."

The added weight of the cell phone in Nikki's fist had contributed greatly to the slight fracture now in Andrea's jaw. As the police car pulled on to Nikki's street and Andrea struggled to her feet, Nikki was relieved to see it was the same two officers that had come the other night. So she had very little explaining to do. They put Andrea into the back of their car again and drove off without even inquiring about her swollen jaw. Nikki drove to the studio to pick up the girls with a smile of satisfaction on her face and her right knuckles throbbing.

CHAPTER 4

Dobs sat at his new desk looking up quotes on his computer for a client he was talking to on the phone. The night before had been a long one and he was tired. Nikki had worn him out again and then they had talked about crazy Andrea until 2AM as they soothed Nikki's hand with an icepack between rounds. He gave the client the quotes he had asked for, said goodbye, and hung up. He was waiting on a return call from Max to get an update after the previous night's altercation between Nikki and Andrea. Certainly the judge would agree to an immediate order, even though Andrea was still locked up from her arrest the night before.

Max called him just before noon. He said the judge would grant the restraining order as soon as she was released from custody. Dobs thanked him for his help, hung up, and called Nikki with the good news.

"Thank God," she responded when he told her.

"So you guys are safe for a while." Dobs wanted to ask her to stay at his place but knew he shouldn't. "So I guess you can go back home now, unless of course you want to stay for a while."

"We might stay one more night. If that's okay?"

"Of course it is. I'll be home about five o'clock. What do you want for dinner?" Dobs thought he might pick something up on the way home.

"Well, the girls are down at the beach right now. I'm picking them up at the end of Main Street about four. Want to eat out? My treat? How about Duke's?" Duke's was a nice restaurant with a cool Hawaiian motif near the pier.

"Sure, sounds good. See you about five." Dobs hung up and got back to work, feeling like everything was going to be okay.

Later, on his way home, he was excited about an evening with Nikki, a relaxed Nikki who wouldn't be so stressed out about the thing with her kids. His phone rang and it was her.

"You are not going to believe this," she began.

"What's wrong now?" Dobs asked.

"I have been looking around for the girls since four o'clock. And they are not here."

"What do you mean?" Dobs asked.

"I mean they are not here. I have the police looking for them too. They are gone. Their cell phones go immediately to voicemail. And no answer to a text." Nikki sounded like she was holding it together better than he ever thought possible.

"Maybe they just lost track of time and ran off with some boys they ran into."

"Oh, that's a lovely thought." Nikki sounded angry now.

"I didn't mean it in a bad way. Maybe they just went for a ride and lost track of time," Dobs offered, trying to calm her down.

"Well, I hope that's what happened. I hope that bitch didn't get out early and come grab them."

"She didn't even know they were in Huntington Beach. I'm sure they are fine. Where should I meet you?"

"In front of Dukes, I guess." Nikki was starting to sound panicky.

Dobs could actually feel his blood pressure rise as he hung up the phone and focused on the traffic. He could not deal with missing children right now, especially Nikki's kids. He began taking some deep breaths, exhaling slowly and saying "I am calm" at the end of each exhalation. He had been instructed on this autogenic relaxation exercise years ago but had never really used it all that much. Now, as he drove down Brookhurst, towards PCH, he wished he had used it more often.

The girls had gone to a friend's house and their cell phones had died. They called Nikki with their explanation. Nikki, both relieved and angry at the same time, asked for an address and told them to be ready in ten minutes. Then she called Dobs and let him know what had happened.

Dobs decided to let Nikki do some mothering and was heading back towards home when he got the call from his attorney, Max Jordash, telling him that the restraining order would not be going through because the judge had decided that no physical threat existed against the two girls or Nikki. They would just have to work it out themselves. Dobs was speechless for a moment while he thought about what Nikki's reaction might be. Then he thanked Max and said goodbye. This was not going to be a great night for Nikki.

Calling her back so soon after they had just talked made Dobs realize that he was getting too involved in this relationship and perhaps he ought to back off a little. When Nikki answered the phone and he told her what his attorney had told him and held his breath while he waited for her to explode. But, she didn't. She calmly said, "Well that's just fucking wonderful, isn't it."

"You definitely ought to bring the girls over tonight? Just to be safe," he offered.

"I know, and we can talk about what options I have. Hey, Dobs, I really appreciate you putting up with all this bullshit, you know that, right?"

"Not a problem," Dobs answered her. "See you about seven-thirty, okay?"

"See you then," Nikki replied.

Dobs thought about what options she might have and came up with nothing as he pressed the end button on his cell phone and pulled into the complex. Just as he was entering the front door, he realized his blood pressure was spiking again.

CHAPTER 4

Dobs walked to his bedroom and took his digital BP monitor out of his bedside table drawer and sat down to take a measurement. It was 190/110. Taking a few deep breaths he walked into the living room and over to the wet bar and poured three fingers of scotch and went into the kitchen for some ice. Then he walked out to the patio and sat down to relax.

Nikki was great. Acknowledged. He probably was falling in love with her. Also true. Which meant that he would have to get involved with protecting her new daughters from the slightly disturbed Andrea. "Great!" he said out loud as he finished his drink and stood up to go make some coffee.

Nikki and the girls arrived at seven-fifteen and they were all seated at Dukes by seven forty-five. During dinner, Dobs tried to make light conversation with Jamie and Allison. But Jamie turned up the dial when she asked him if Allison's Mom would want to take her too, even though she wasn't her real mother.

Dobs looked at Nikki before he answered Jamie. "I don't think anyone is going to be taking anybody, Jamie. This woman had fifteen years to decide if she wanted to be Allison's mother and apparently never decided it was that important. So now, Nikki here is your Mom. Let's just forget about this other woman if we can."

Allison said, "Yeah, right. Just forget about it." She looked at Jamie as she spoke.

Nikki said, "Well do you want me to set up a meeting with her? Just to see if you want her to be your Mom or not?"

"I don't think that would be a very good idea." Dobs looked into Nikki's eyes as he spoke. "It could complicate things even more."

"Yeah," Nikki began, "but it could also clear some things up, right? Allison could then decide if she wanted to be with me or not."

"But this woman has some serious issues, right? You sure you want to have a sit down meeting with her? I think it's a bad idea. But it's your decision." Dobs took a drink of red wine and decided to stop talking for a minute or two.

"Well, if Allison wants to meet her I can't really say no to the idea. I mean, I'm sure you want to meet your birth mother, who wouldn't?" Nikki looked at Allison. "And if you decide to go with her that's your decision. Of course, the court will have some say in it but if I agree they might let you go with her."

"But I just wanted to talk with her. I'm not saying I want to live with her!" Allison offered. "Just to see what she is like, you know."

Dobs was staring across the room when he saw her. "Well you just might get your chance, sweetie." Then he looked at Nikki and said, "She is standing over by the bar."

Nikki turned and saw Andrea talking to the bartender. "Oh my God'" she exclaimed softly. "It is her. What should we do?"

"Coming our way," Dobs announced as he took a drink of his wine.

"Well Good Evening everyone," began Andrea, rubbing her jaw before turning to the girls. "And hello girls." Then she stared at Allison, saying "Hi Honey. You do know I am your mother right? And I have been trying to find you for so long."

Dobs suggested, "Have a seat." Nikki kicked him under the table.

Andrea sat down next to Allison and started stroking her hair as she spoke. "I can't believe I finally found you. Please tell me you want to come home with me."

Allison nervously shook her head no, saying, "Not really, but we can talk some if you want to."

"Can we get some privacy?" Andrea asked as she stood up again. "We can just go sit over there in the bar. Don't worry. You'll still be able to see her. We just want to talk." Allison stood up and walked over to the bar with her mother. Nikki just sat there, frozen.

"I can not believe this is happening!" she said to Dobs. "I mean, there is nothing I can do to stop this, correct?"

"Correct. Unless she begins to be a threat to you or the girls." Dobs finished his wine and signaled for the waiter to bring another one. "Just let them talk for a few minutes and we will leave."

Thirty minutes later Dobs stood up and walked over to the table in the bar. "We are leaving now."

"Allison might be coming to my place for a sleep-over," Andrea offered gleefully.

"Is that right Allison?"

"No, not tonight." Allison stood up. "But we can get together and talk again sometime if you like."

Dobs put his hand on Allison's shoulder and they said goodbye to Andrea, turned to walk back to their table, and then headed out the door without another word being said. The drive home was quiet and when they got to Dobs' condo the girls went to bed and Nikki and Dobs sat out on the patio and said very little to each other. Nikki was right. There was nothing she could do about it, for now.

CHAPTER 5

After a few rough moments between Nikki and Andrea, Allison began to see her mother every few days after school. Nikki had agreed to it because Allison really wanted to do it. When the weekend came that Allison asked if she could stay over with her mother, Nikki agreed to it, against her better judgment.

Dobs had been distant about the whole thing lately, after initially expressing support for Nikki's decision to let the woman see her daughter. He made sure Nikki understood she could lose her but she really had no choice. She could still keep Jamie. But Allison might just decide to go with her mother.

On the Sunday afternoon of the sleepover visit with Andrea, Allison called and said she was ready to come home. She needed to talk to Nikki about the situation. She was considering moving in with Andrea.

Dobs held Nikki as she sobbed but she was actually pretty strong about it. She had braced herself for this to happen. The following Monday she would contact the adoption agency and find out what needed to be done. Dobs convinced her to wait a week or so and make sure things went well first.

Dobs wanted to ask Nikki to move in with him. But it was too far from her club and there was the whole thing with Paul dropping by all the time. Dobs began to call her a little less often, giving her space. He wanted to spend some time with his own daughter before she got married and that's what he set out to do.

Dawn answered her cell with a great big "Hey Dad, how's your love life?" She loved to kid him about the new girlfriend she still hadn't met.

"She's fine, listen. Why don't you and me and your husband-to-be head over to Catalina. It's on me. We can spend the night and come back the next day."

"Sounds awesome. This coming weekend?"

"Yeah."

"Okay, I will talk to him and call you back. Love you." She ended the call before he even said goodbye.

It was Tuesday evening and Dobs decided to drive down to the ocean for dinner alone at Harpoon Harry's. He loved their shrimp and needed a nice quiet break from it all.

While Dobs sat quietly enjoying his meal, Andrea was frantically trying to get Allison to help her practice some ballet out in the back yard of her home in Lake

Forest. She had forgotten to take her meds again but was so intensely focused on the dancing that she didn't realize how extreme her behavior was becoming.

"Now Alli, just do what I do," she was saying sternly. Allison looked like she had absolutely no desire to do what her mother wanted her to do. She stood there with her hands on her hips staring at her half-crazed mother.

"Mom, if you want me to come live with you...." Allison began. "I mean, seriously. I think the neighbors are staring at you at this point." Tchaikovsky blasted out through the patio speakers.

Andrea grabbed Alli's hand and began pumping it up and down in time with the music as she kicked her legs wildly, one by one, into the air. "Dance my darling!"

Alli dropped her hand and stepped back a few paces from her mother, watching as Andrea went into a wild finale before finally collapsing into the grass at her feet. "Very nice, Mom. Can we go inside now?"

Andrea looked up at her and shook her head no, saying "practice, practice, practice" is what we need to do. "Come on. Give me your hand again."

"I am going inside now. You have fun out here." Alli glanced over at the neighbors who were watching her mother from their deck as she walked back to the house.

Living with her mother was going to be too bizarre. She had already decided to stay with Nikki and Jamie but was just trying to give her mother some more time. She had seen the bipolar episodes up close and she knew she would not be able to handle it for very long. But after all, this was her mother and she needed to spend some time with her.

She had missed all the little things a girl gets to do with a mom. Playing dress up, learning to use makeup, baking cookies and making lemonade for a lemonade stand, reading Harry Potter together at night before bed. Now she just wanted to have a little bit of that back, if possible.

Andrea sat in the grass and stared up at Alli, smiling. She thought back to when she was that age, living up in Santa Cruz, in the mountains, with her parents. They lived in a small ranch style home that hung over a small cliff defying the earth to produce a seismic jolt that would knock them down. She was a junior in high school when her mother told her it would not be right to go to school pregnant and so she had dropped out and stayed home to have the baby. Baby Allison. As she looked up at her now she smiled broadly, which emphasized her high cheek bones, and said, "Alli, let's take a little trip up to Santa Cruz. I want to show you where I grew up. Where you were born."

Alli stared back at her mother sitting in the grass and did not answer at first, finally saying, "Sure, I guess." Her mother jumped up and walked over to her for a hug, talking quickly about how much fun they would have up there as they both walked back towards the house.

That night she told Alli about her birth when Andrea was only sixteen years old, how they had used a nurse midwife and she had been delivered at home. Hearing the story gave Alli a sense of peace. She began to understand why her mother had turned her over for adoption.

She would probably do the same thing if she became pregnant in high school, thinking of the *Babies having Babies* video they had watched in health class a few weeks earlier.

"Mom," Alli began. "You know I really do want to be a part of your life, right?"

"Of course I know that."

"Well, I also want to be a part of Nikki's life. So how are we going to work that out?"

"We will work it out sweetie. But for now, we are packing our bags for Santa Cruz."

"Did you take your meds?" Alli asked her, suspicious of this manic behavior about leaving right now.

"Yes I took my pills." Andrea turned and walked towards her room. "Now I've got a small suitcase in here that you can use."

"How long are we going to be gone?" Alli asked her mom.

"Don't worry about school. I'll call you in for the next few days, say you have the flu or something. It'll be just fine."

"And what about Nikki?"

"Tell her we are going to visit your birthplace and we will be back on Thursday." Andrea was packing as she spoke.

"She is not going to be very happy with that, you know."

"Oh well, it is what it is." She continued packing.

"Guess I will give her a call. She still is my legal guardian, you know that, right?"

"I know, I know. For now at least."

Allison walked out to the front yard and placed the call to Nikki while Andrea was packing and singing in the back bedroom.

Nikki was just getting ready to head home from her studio when she got the call. For the last few days she had sunk into a deep depression she couldn't shake. When Alli told her she would be back on Friday and would be missing a few days of school, it was as though she had almost expected more bad news. "That's fine. Not like I have much say in the matter, unless I call the police as your legal guardian but then that would screw up your little reunion. So just be safe and come back on time. And give me name, number, and an address for where you will be." She paused. "I love you Allison and I want the best for you."

"I know. I love you too. But I just have to do this thing and I hope you understand." Allison told Nikki she would text the info later, said good bye, and walked back in to tell Andrea she would be going with her.

Andrea's minivan was a vintage 1972 type 2 VW bus. She had spent thousands having it brought up to mint condition and once she got behind the wheel on the open road she was in her own world. She blasted the Beatles White Album from the stereo system so loud that she and Alli said very little to each other that evening as they drove up to Santa Cruz.

They got there about ten-thirty and Andrea turned off the engine and the lights as she coasted into the long gravel driveway of her parent's home. "We are going to surprise them!" She remembered using this engine and lights off technique to sneak out of the house at night back when she still lived there. Now she beamed maniacally as she used the same technique to surprise her Mom and Dad. "Come on, but be quiet."

They walked up to the front steps of the old brick, stone and log home that rested precariously on the edge of the mountain. They were at about 2000 feet elevation but the drop from where the home had been built thirty years earlier was only about 200 feet. It was supported by giant pine logs that had once been trees surrounding the property. They had been wedged into the rock to secure the back of the home and create a porch like edge overlooking the valley below. Andrea held her breath as she knocked on the door.

Her mother looked old and tired as she answered the door, saying "Andi, is that you?" as she looked at her daughter and the teenaged girl standing next to her.

"Yes Mom, it's me. And this is your granddaughter, Allison. May we come in?" she asked in a kidding way as she walked in and gave her mother a hug.

Andrea walked in to the foyer and greeted her mother with a hug, followed by Allison doing the same thing. "Where's Pop?" Andrea asked as she looked around the warm, cozy living room that brought back so many memories for her.

"He's out back," her mother responded.

"Out back?" Andrea asked, remembering nothing out back except the yard strewn with boulders that led up to the side of a mountain.

"Yes, he stays out there now."

"What do you mean he stays out there?"

"In his hut. He built a little cottage last summer. It's actually quite nice. He ran heat out there too so its nice and comfortable for him."

"I don't understand. He sleeps out there too?" Andrea looked puzzled.

"Sometimes out, sometimes inside. Depends on his mood. He built himself kind of a mini observatory in the hut. The roof opens up a bit and he spends hours with his telescope staring at distant worlds."

"Is he okay, Mom? I mean…."

"Yeah. He's fine. Just loves looking at the stars." Her mother paused and glanced over at Allison.

"But we must bring him inside to meet his granddaughter!" She turned and began walking towards the rear of the home. Allison gave Andrea a puzzled look as they followed her into the kitchen. When Andrea's mother walked out the kitchen door, Andrea and Allison stayed inside exchanging nervous glances.

"This feels kind of weird, Mom." Allison said, just as Andrea's father walked in through the kitchen door.

He was in his sixties and wore his gray hair down to his shoulders. He squinted and peered at the two of them as his bloodshot eyes got used to the light. He was wearing a bathrobe that was barely closed in the front and it appeared that he might have nothing on underneath the robe.

Allison moved closer to Andrea, fearfully putting her arm around her waist as she said, "Hello, Grandpa."

"Hi Dad, how you doing?" Andrea broke away from Allison and gave the old man a hug.

"I'm real good," he answered her. "And this is my granddaughter? What's you name, hon?"

"I'm Alli." She held out her hand. "It's a real pleasure to meet you."

Grandpa moved towards her, tightening the belt on his robe as he did so. He embraced her in a big hug. Allison was aware of a smell she had never smelled before as he held on to her tightly and kissed her on her ear while his head rested on her shoulder.

Freeing herself from his embrace she turned to her mother. "Where is our room, Mom? I'm feeling kind of tired."

"Nonsense," said her Grandmom. "I need to catch up. I'll make coffee."

"I'll stay up with you Mom," said Andrea. "Alli you can go bed down if you want to, if you are really that tired."

"Thanks Mom." Alli stood nervously waiting for someone to give her directions to the bedroom.

Andrea moved towards her and held her hand. "Let me show you my old bedroom. We'll sleep in there."

Saying goodnight to her grandparents Alli followed her Mom down the hall to the bedroom. There were psychedelic posters on the walls and the room had a double bed. One window looked out over the front yard and Andrea pulled the curtain shut and turned on the bedside table lamp. "Now you get comfortable. The bathroom is right across the hall and I'll go get our bags from the van. Be right back."

Alli stared at the posters and then walked into the bathroom to wash her face. As she looked at herself in the mirror she wished she was back at home with Nikki and Jamie. Standing in the bathroom doorway, it struck her that this was the house she was born in. Her mother had explained that a midwife had come and helped with the delivery. She walked back into the bedroom. Was this the room where she first took a breath?

She heard coughing and a rough voice from down the hall asking, "Where did our girl go to now? She can't be turning in already." It was Grandpa.

Looking back into the bedroom and walking in towards the bed, Allison began to feel lightheaded. She wanted to call Nikki. Something didn't feel right here and she wanted to go home.

Just as she pulled her cell phone out of her pocket, her mother walked into the room. "What are you doing in here, Allison? Grandpa wants to see you. Can you come on out for just a few minutes before you turn in?"

Allison told her she would be right out and Andrea walked back towards the kitchen. Then she quickly opened up her phone and called Nikki, who answered on the second ring.

"Allison, are you okay?" Just hearing Nikki's voice made her feel so much better.

"I miss you guys." Allison hesitated before continuing. "And I want to come home."

"You are at your grandparent's house in Santa Cruz, correct?" Nikki asked.

"Right."

"And can you get me the street address?" Nikki was methodical. "Tell them you need to get something out of the car and get me the address from the front of the house."

Allison was staring at a small desk in the corner of the room as she spoke with Nikki. A stack of mail was on the edge of the desk. She stood up and walked over to get an envelope and read the address to Nikki. "227 Holly Ridge Way, Santa Cruz."

Just as she set the envelope back down again she heard Andrea coming back down the hall. Nikki told her she would be there in the morning to pick her up and she would call her before she pulled up.

"Are you coming out to visit with Grandpa or not?" Andrea sounded like this was going to be a truly fun thing to do.

"I'm coming." Allison put the phone back in her pocket and followed Andrea back to the kitchen. Grandpa sat on a straight backed kitchen chair, his robe cracked open just enough to show too much.

"Come give your Grandpa a hug." He held his arms out and waited for her to come to him.

Slowly and reluctantly she walked across the room and gave him a hug without coming too close to his body, which still had a foul smell to it, as though he hadn't bathed in a while.

Andrea took the lead in starting the conversation. "So, Dad, you built yourself an observatory? You have a passion for stargazing all of a sudden?"

Grandpa scratched himself as he answered. "Astronomy. I love it. Bought the scope online and made the adjustments to the hut so I could slide back the roof and stay warm while I observed." He stood up and tightened his robe. "Come on, both of you. I'll show you. Saturn is out tonight." He walked towards the back door and they all followed.

The cottage, or "hut", was big enough for the four of them as long as they all sat on the bed. Grandpa sat on a barstool below the telescope and lined it up for them to see. "Come here Allison. You take the first look." He grinned like a young boy as he spoke to her.

Allison stood up and walked over to the telescope and Grandpa climbed off the stool and patted it to indicate she should sit down on it. As soon as she placed her eye in front of the eyepiece, a radiant Saturn and its rings were floating majestically in the center of the lens. She had never seen anything like it. It was so beautiful. She watched as she heard the soft hum of the telescope's motor gently turn to keep the planet in its field of view. This was indeed quite a setup her grandfather had, she thought to herself, just as she felt his hand come to rest on her back.

It was dark in the hut and Andrea and her mother could not see much as they waited for their turn at the telescope, but Allison could feel Grandpa's hand as it softly made its way around her side and brushed up against her left breast. She turned immediately to the right and hopped off the stool as she said, "Now I am ready for bed. That was really, really cool Grandpa." She walked out the door of the hut and back inside the house and headed straight for her bedroom, where she climbed under the covers and tried to fall asleep, clutching her cell phone in the palm of her hand.

CHAPTER 5

She was awakened six hours later by the vibrating of her phone still clutched tightly in her hand. Nikki would be pulling up in five minutes. Allison realized her mother was not in bed with her. Maybe she had gotten up earlier, or maybe she had slept on the couch. Anyway, Allison jumped out of bed and quietly made it to the bathroom. It was about 6AM and she couldn't hear that anyone else awake as she quietly washed her face and toweled off. She knew she should tell her mother she was leaving but she didn't want to cause a scene. She would call from the road.

She walked out the front door quietly and walked down towards the street just as she saw the headlights of Nikki's car turn on to her street. Nikki pulled up quietly and turned off her lights as soon as she saw Allison. The sun was starting to rise and she didn't really need the lights to see anymore.

Allison ran around to the passenger side and got in. Jamie was asleep in the back seat. She hugged Nikki and said, "Let's just go. Hurry, before she comes out here."

They pulled away quietly and Allison began to tell Nikki about Grandpa and how weird everything had been the night before. She thanked her for driving up to get her, asking, "How come Dobs didn't come along?"

"I left as soon as we hung up. No time to get him. We'll see him later today. He was very concerned about you when I told him you had called." Nikki yawned.

"Let me drive for while so you can sleep?" Allison suggested, even though she had only recently received her learner's permit.

"Sounds wonderful," said Nikki as she pulled over to the side of the road. "I need to close my eyes. Just keep going south on this highway and wake me up in an hour and please, do not speed. Thank you. And I love you."

Allison adjusted the seat and sent a short text message to Andrea to let her know she was okay and on her way back home. She turned off her cell phone and slowly pulled back on to the highway just as she saw Nikki closing her eyes. Allison said, "I love you too, Nikki."

CHAPTER 6

Dobs was pacing in front of his desk as he talked to a client about the savage beating the market was taking but all he could think about was Nikki. She had told him late last night she was on her way to pick up Allison and even though he had offered to come along she had refused, saying she would take care of it herself and see him when she got back. He didn't know what had gone wrong, only that Allison had called and asked her to come pick her up.

After work he drove to Nikki's place and saw that she was back and knew she must be sleeping. He thought about going home but decided against it. He knocked on the door and Allison answered it, rubbing her eyes. She had been sleeping on the sofa in the living room. Nikki was in her bedroom, still asleep. Dobs asked Allison if she was okay and she shook her head and said, "Yeah, I'm good. Just tired."

He walked towards the hallway, saying, "I'm just going to look in on her. You can go back to sleep."

Nikki's lovely face lay sideways on her pillow and he could tell she was in a deep sleep. Dobs just watched her for a few minutes and then turned to leave the room. Then he heard her say, "Where do you think you're going?"

He climbed in bed with her and she told him what had happened up in Santa Cruz. He sat up, saying, "Her grandfather actually groped her?"

"Sounds like that's what happened. Plus she felt really uncomfortable there anyway. She wants to stay with me now. Thank God." Nikki sat up on the edge of the bed and yawned. "At least I got some sleep. And I am starving."

"Wherever you guys want to go, just say the word." Dobs put his hand on her shoulder and turned her to face him and kissed her on the forehead. "You've had one hell of a day." He stood up and stretched. "Should we ask the girls where they want to eat?"

Nikki answered him just as the sound of screeching tires could be heard from the front of the house. Looking out her bedroom window she could see it was Andrea's van. Without any hesitation she reached for her phone and dialed 911. "I am through playing games with this crazy bitch."

After she hung up she reached in her bedside table drawer for a small 38 caliber revolver she kept there for safety. She marched towards the front of the house and stopped once to face Dobs. "Please keep the girls in the back of the house until I get rid of her."

Dobs stared dumbly at her as she left the room, gun in hand. He jumped up and followed her out and got Allison from the living room and took her back to Jamie's room before she could tell what was going on. Jamie was on the computer when they walked in and Dobs closed the bedroom door and sat down on the edge of Jamie's bed.

Nikki opened the front door and stared directly into Andrea's face as she spoke, keeping the gun hidden behind her back. "Now listen to me, bitch. The police are on their way. Your father groped Allison's breasts while he was showing her the planets through his telescope. So get back into your pathetic little van, leave here now, and don't ever come back, or you can spend the rest of the night explaining the whole thing to the cops."

Andrea stood there listening and tears formed in her eyes. "I have no idea what you are talking about. Can I please see Allison?"

"No, now leave here. Right now." Nikki's hand held the revolver tightly behind her back as she said it more forcefully. "Right now. I already called 911."

Andrea put her head down for a minute and then quickly turned to leave. She climbed into the van and drove away only a minute before the police arrived.

Nikki hid the gun behind the door and walked outside to greet the police. She told them it was a false alarm, that the same woman who had been stalking her kids had come by but she had forced her to leave. She thanked them profusely before walking back inside and closing the door.

She picked up the revolver and carried it back to her bedroom. Then she went into Jamie's room and asked the girls if they had decided where they wanted to eat dinner.

"They want Lamppost Pizza," Dobs announced. "And we're ready when you are!"

"Be ready in ten minutes," Nikki said as she walked out of the room and back to her bedroom, thinking about what she should do about what had happened to Allison. If she reported it to the police in Santa Cruz it would be a long drawn out court deal, and Allison would have to go testify. If she said nothing maybe the crazy lady would leave them alone and that's the plan she decided upon as she finished getting dressed.

While Dobs, Nikki, Allison, and Jamie were enjoying their pizza at Lamppost, Andrea was randomly driving around Orange County as she cried and talked to herself. She did not understand what had happened, but she remembered her father had often touched her girlfriends inappropriately when she was a teenager and had a few friends over. She never thought much of it because her friends just laughed it off. But apparently Allison was not laughing it off.

She had to take care of Allison. She was convinced it was something she had to do. But now, she realized she must take her by force and run away with her if she was going to get her at all. As she drove down Newport Boulevard it occurred to her that there was one more option. If something were to happen to Nikki, especially if something were to happen before she was able to say anything to anyone about what had happened to Allison, she could simply just petition the court for custody. After all, Allison was her daughter. As she stared at the traffic through her tears, she felt a sense of relief. She now had a plan.

But she would have to talk to her brother, Jake. He would know someone who could help her. She hadn't talked to him in over a year but now she knew she had to see him. She decided to drive up to San Pedro and see if she could find him. She knew the bar where he used to hang out. She would start there.

The last time she saw Jake he was strung out on meth. He had worked a back table at a waterfront tavern called Sunny's Place in San Pedro. She had tried to do an intervention and get him into NA but he had laughed at her, humiliated her in front of his friends, and then asked her to leave the place since she was obviously too good for the rest of them. She had run out in tears. The Jake she remembered from childhood was gone and in his place was an evil man. But that's what she needed now. And she had some cash that might sway him into helping her. Cash she had been saving from the sales of her artwork to help raise her daughter and maybe send her to college.

She pulled up in front of Sunny's Place and parked her van along the sidewalk out front. If there was such a thing as a Happy Hour at Sunny's, this is what Andrea walked in on. Several bikers were shooting pool and a Bryan Adams song played loudly through the sound system. A couple of gals who were probably hookers sat at the bar and about half the tables were full of customers, seedy looking customers. Andrea walked up to the bartender and said, "I'm looking for Jake."

The bartender scratched his head and continued drying off a beer mug he had washed, answering her, "Who wants to know?"

"I'm his sister." Andrea stared into the tired man's eyes.

"Oh, I see." He turned away from her to put the mug on the shelf behind him as he continued. "Jake got busted. You didn't hear?"

"No, we haven't talked in a while."

"Yeah. He's out on bail now, keeping a low profile."

"Where's he staying?" Andrea was hoping to get an answer but knew she probably wouldn't.

"Actually he's staying right down the street with some gal he's been shacking up with." The bartender acted like he wanted to help her now.

"You have an address or a number?" she asked eagerly.

"No, but leave me your number and I'll give it to him when he comes in."

Andrea pulled one of her ARTIST FOR HIRE business cards out of her purse and handed it to him. "Tell him it's urgent. I need to talk to him."

"You got it sweetie." He looked at the name on her card and added, "I mean 'Andrea'."

"Thank you." Andrea turned and walked out to the street again. She stopped in front of her van and decided to take a short walk up and down the street while there was still some daylight left. She reached into her purse and took her pills out and took one of them. She knew she must not forget to take them, not now. Too much to get done.

She remembered a small art studio that used to be around the corner from Sunny's so she decided to stroll down and see if it was still there. As she walked she thought back to the time she first came to San Pedro. It was a Saturday afternoon in 1994, and she was tripping on LSD with a friend of hers. They had dropped the acid in Seal Beach early one Saturday morning and had somehow ended up in San Pedro. Some guys had picked them up and brought them there in a VW minibus. They had wandered and stumbled around Fort MacArthur, a WW1 training facility that still had huge, empty artillery batteries, which were said by some to be the site of paranormal activity. She remembered how her friend had thought this would be a fantastic place to trip. Andrea's memory of the whole thing was vague, with no recollection of the floating orbs and footsteps her friend had claimed to witness.

This is where she had first met Ron, who would soon become Allison's father. He was one of the guys that had picked them up. He was about ten years older than her, maybe twenty five or so. He looked like a real hippie too, and that did it for Andrea. She had always felt like she should have been a flower child in the sixties and had kept the right posters on her wall at home and listened to the old sixties and seventies music all the time. When she first saw the shirtless Ron with his long blond hair and cutoff jeans and sandals, she fell for him.

Her friend, Gail, had run off with Ron's friend, leaving the two of them to explore the empty WW1 catacombs and tunnels that had been closed to the public for years. She thought that somewhere in this place of cold dark concrete and silent ghostly murmurings might be the place where Allison had been conceived that night.

As she turned the corner she saw that the art studio was no longer there. In its place was a small convenience store. She turned around and headed back to her van, thinking about how much she wanted Alli to live with her and hoping that Jake would call her soon.

CHAPTER 7

Dobs, Nikki, Allison, and Jamie all sat on oversized beach towels near Lifeguard Stand 24 at Bolsa Chica State Beach in Huntington Beach. Dobs liked this spot much more than down by the pier on Main Street. This was actually a state park on the beach: nice restrooms, dressing rooms, concession stand, and, best of all, fire pits on the beach! He had stopped to buy fire wood and even though it was still late afternoon he had already claimed their pit simply by sitting next to it. And there were staffed lifeguard towers every hundred yards. If the Pacific's undertow caught anyone in its grip these guys and gals were on it immediately. A perfect spot for a family, Dobs thought to himself as he looked lovingly at Nikki and the two girls.

It was a Sunday afternoon and they had all agreed that it was time for a day at the beach. The girls didn't even complain about not being close to the Main Street shops. A Jack-in-the-Box stood a short distance away from where they sat, right outside the park's rear exit gate. They would have Jumbo Jacks, shakes, and curly fires for dinner and then watch the sunset as the fire pit's flames kept them warm.

Dobs was relieved that the whole issue with Allison's mother finally appeared to be over. A week had passed since Nikki had chased the mother away from her house and they had not heard anymore from her. Things were settling down nicely.

A few nights before he had introduced Nikki and the girls to his daughter and her fiancé, and that too had gone very well. Nikki spent her evenings at her house but Dobs slept over a lot. As he looked at the sun going down and the orange sky surrounding it, he realized he had not been this happy in years.

"Nikki," he began, "do you really think the whole thing with Alli is all over now?

"That crazy bitch," Nikki mumbled to herself. "It better be over."

"So what if she comes back to the house looking for her?" Dobs asked.

"She won't. She knows her father would be in trouble if she did that. I really think it's all over." Nikki stretched out in the sand and watched the two girls roasting marshmallows over the fire pit. She reached into her bag and pulled out a bottle of red wine. Knowing it was illegal on the beach she asked him, "Dare we?"

CHAPTER 7

Dobs grabbed the bottle and an opener she held and quickly opened and poured the entire bottle into an empty plastic Big Gulp cup one of the girls had been using earlier. "I think we will be just fine." He dug a hole in the sand and buried the bottle and the cork before turning to her again. "There. Evidence is gone."

"That's a lot of wine to drink, Dobs." Nikki smiled at him.

"Yeah, it is." He took a drink from the cup before passing it to her. "We'll be here for a while, correct?"

"Correct." Nikki took a drink and handed the cup back to him. "I just can't believe what has happened in the last few weeks."

"You mean with us?" Dobs asked.

"No, with Allison and her mother. Can you?"

"Well, I suppose she wants to get her daughter back. I even suspect she is not through trying."

"She can keep trying if she likes and go visit her father in prison. In a way it was really a blessing that the old man went after Alli. It bought me protection. Know what I mean?" Nikki took another large drink of wine.

"Yeah, I suppose."

"So you really think she'll try again?" Nikki asked.

"Unfortunately, I do. Too bad you couldn't get that restraining order. That would have helped things."

"Yeah, well, I have my own restraining order now," she said as she patted the revolver in her beach bag. Then, looking out to the dark sea, she added, "Bitch."

Later that evening at Nikki's house, after the girls were in bed, he approached Nikki from behind and placed his hands on her shoulder, gently turning her around to face him. As he looked into her eyes he felt a growing love for her, more than the usual lust he had felt initially. "You know," he began, "we do make quite a team."

"I know," Nikki said. "That we do."

"And the girls really like me a lot, right?" Dobs asked.

"Yeah, they do. Why, where are you going with this Dobs?" Nikki's tone was suspicious.

"Oh, I just had a really good time today with you guys." He wanted to say more, tell her that he felt like he was falling in love with her, but he didn't. "You had a good time too, right?"

"Of course I did silly. What a nice spot that was. We've never been there. Always went to Newport or Balboa." Nikki looked up at him. "You about ready for bed, big guy?"

"You bet." He kissed her and she led him towards her bedroom. Calm fell over the house as the lights were turned off.

The next morning Dobs woke up early and drove to his place to change for work. He kissed Nikki goodbye while she was still sound asleep. He quietly locked the front door and tried not to wake up the girls.

Once at the office, his day became full of earnings reports and client phone calls, so when his phone rang at three-thirty he was surprised to hear Paul's voice on the other end of the line when he answered. "This is Dobs."

"It's me, Paul." It was Nikki's assistant and he was upset.

"What's wrong?" Dobs rubbed his forehead as he heard the news.

"Nikki has been hurt." Paul stopped. "Someone ran into her as she was crossing PCH. She is at Hoag in ICU."

Dobs sat stunned at his desk. "What do you mean? How…."

"Hit with a truck, Dobs. They ran over her as she was crossing the street and never stopped."

"So they don't know who did it?"

"Correct."

"How are the girls?"

"The police called Child Protection Services and they came over and picked them up about fifteen minutes ago. They had just come home from school. Fortunately they never saw Nikki's body. It was pretty bad. The girls were still at school when it happened."

"Thank you Paul. I will be there in fifteen minutes. Are you at the hospital?"

"Yes, I am here." Paul's voice was full of his sadness.

Dobs began to cry as he walked out of the office towards the parking lot. He got into his car and felt like he wasn't really there at all. He started the car and drove out of the lot, tears streaming down his cheeks.

Once he arrived at Hoag Hospital the tears had been replaced with anger. Paul was seated in the main lobby. His Schwarzenegger stature and physique looked somewhat smaller today. His head was buried in his hands.

"How could this have happened, Paul? She was way too careful to be hit by a truck. Right?"

"Yeah, I guess so. But that's what they say happened."

"Listen to me, Paul. This thing might not have been an accident." Dobs had been thinking about it, how unlikely it was that Nikki would have been hit by a truck crossing the street. "Don't you see? I think that Allison's birth mother had something to do with this. I am going to talk to the police about it."

Paul sat with his head in his hands. "I guess you might be right. I just don't get it though." He rubbed his eyes and stood up from the table. "The police asked me if she had a boyfriend or husband and I told them about you. You'll probably be hearing from them soon enough. I gotta get out of here for now. See you." Paul walked towards the door. "Sure would be nice if you could take care of those girls for her. She really does care about them you know."

"I know she does Paul. I will do what I can." Dobs watched as Paul walked out the door. Dobs headed for the elevators.

Once on the ICU floor, the charge nurse told him he couldn't see Nikki yet. Maybe later that evening. He did learn that she might be paralyzed from the waist down and that she was in a coma. He told her he wanted to wait and she directed him to a small waiting room at the end of the hall.

After reading an old Time magazine article he began to doze off, only to be awakened by the sound of two men in suits walking into the waiting room. They were Newport Beach Detectives. The tall thin one introduced himself as Detective Boyle and said, "Okay if we ask you a few questions?"

The shorter detective put a small recording device on the end table and asked, "You mind if I record this interview, Mr. Dobson?"

"Not at all. I actually have a theory on what might have happened to Nikki."

Detective Boyle spoke, "Oh really? We would love to hear about it."

Dobs explained what had been happening with Allison's birth mother over the last few weeks and how Nikki had chased her away from the house the week before and told her never to return. He even told them about the Grandpa incident. When he was done they asked a few more questions and he told them where he had been all day. His alibi was solid since everyone at the office would say he had been there. He didn't feel like a suspect but he knew it was important to let them know where he had been. Then they could eliminate him and focus on Andrea. But he didn't have Andrea's last name. He could only tell them that if they checked the police records from the last few weeks they would see she had been picked up in front of Nikki's house for harassment.

The detectives asked a few more questions and then they left him alone again, offering him their sympathy and telling him to "hang in there."

While Dobs sat in the waiting room musing about his life's dramatic turn of events, Nikki regained consciousness in the ICU. She slowly opened her eyes and became aware of the sounds of the machines next to her bed that were pumping fluids and emitting soft erratic beeps as they kept her alive. The pain in her right shoulder where the truck had initially impacted her was radiating all the way down her back. But that was it. It stopped about two thirds of the way down her back and from below where it stopped she felt nothing. She tried to move her legs but could not.

She was able to press the call button with her right hand and within a few seconds a short, dark haired nurse came through the door. "You are awake? Thank goodness. Let me get your doctor."

Nikki felt like she was not quite awake, but she was conscious and felt the effects of the drugs they were pumping into her. She closed her eyes and thought about Allison and Jamie. Were they home from school yet? Did they know she was in the hospital? Then her thoughts turned to the truck that had hit her and the driver's face as he plowed right into her. But that was all she could remember just as the doctor entered the room.

"Hello there, I am Dr. Muranda." He was soft-spoken, in his mid fifties, and of medium height. His hand rubbed his balding head as he asked, "Miss Pittilon, I need to ask you some questions. First, can you feel your legs at all?"

Nikki tried to feel her legs and could not. She touched her hips with her hands but could not feel her hands on her legs, as though she were touching someone else's legs under the covers. "No," she answered. "I can not feel my legs. Is it permanent?"

"Too early to say, but maybe. The spinal MRI showed extensive damage but we must just wait and see how you do." He wrote something in her chart.

"Can I see my girls?" Nikki asked.

"No, but they are being well taken care of."

"By who?"

"The authorities had to call Child Protective Services while you were in a coma." The doctor looked down at the chart as he spoke.

"What?" Nikki tried to scream, but it didn't come out very loud. "What do you mean? Call them and tell them I am out of the coma. Get them back for me. Where is Dobs anyway?"

"Who?" The doctor asked, just as the nurse walked over to him and whispered into his ear. "Oh, you must mean your friend. He is in the waiting room. I will send him in to see you." Dr. Muranda turned and walked out of the room, saying, "We will be running more tests tomorrow for your spine. Just rest for now. Your children are fine."

Nikki closed her eyes and started to pray. She was still praying when Dobs walked in and said, "Hey you."

Nikki opened her eyes. "They have the girls in custody. You must get them out for me." Her eyes were wet with tears as she spoke.

"Of course I will. You just relax. I am going down to the courts first thing in the morning. Of course, they may not let them come with me you know. It's not like I am your husband. But I am going to try. Do you have any close relatives I can call? Maybe that would help."

"Maybe you should go down now. Are they still open?" She had no idea what time it was and the courts were closed. "I have an Aunt over in Riverside. Paul has her number. Maybe she could go to court with you. She was my mother's sister and she has met the girls on several occasions. Maybe that will help. Oh God, I can't believe this is happening." She reached out and grabbed his arm. "Dobs, I can not feel my legs." The water in her eyes began to run down her cheeks.

CHAPTER 8

Andrea drove into the parking lot at the government building in Orange and checked her appearance quickly in the rear view mirror before getting out of her van. This was a very big day for her. She was here to petition the court for custody of Allison, and she had decided to also take Jamie if they let her. And why wouldn't they let her? They were back into the system now that their foster mother was incapacitated.

It was Tuesday morning and she knew she had to act quickly. The girls had only been in custody since the previous afternoon, and when the detectives visited her the night before she was absolutely sure they had suspected nothing. They had asked her a few questions and she had told them she was very sorry about Nikki's accident but that her first duty was to get her daughter back.

As she walked up the Orange County government office building steps she didn't recognize Dobs, who had also decided to try and get temporary custody of the girls. He was entering the front doors of the building and had not seen Andrea on the steps far below him.

He went to the room number he had been told to go to, walked in and sat down in a large waiting area, and waited to speak to someone. When Andrea walked in a few minutes later he recognized her but she did not recognize him. She sat on the far side of the room sketching something on a small pad while she also waited.

Her mind raced into the future as she drew a picture of a small house she would be living in with the two girls, probably somewhere in Nevada or Arizona. The prices were good there and she could get a nice place cheap. She would have a room for her painting and be close to a major airport for the occasional out of town wedding portrait that paid so well. And the girls could go to a nice school with top ratings. She would check it all out on the GreatSchools.com website. Get the scores. Know what area she would need to live in. She would leave immediately if the court gave her custody. No one could find them and they would be safe. And if she didn't get custody? Well, she could be patient and just wait.

Dobs was first to get to see the caseworker, Mrs. Johnson. He explained everything that had happened and told her that Nikki's Aunt would also be available to help with the kids until Nikki was better. He told her about Andrea and how dangerous he felt she was.

He gave the caseworker Detective Boyle's name and number and told her she could call him to confirm what he had just told her.

Mrs. Johnson told him that the girls were fine and that they would be allowed to visit Nikki as soon as the doctor said it was okay. This was great news. As far as their living arrangements, she was willing to let them go back to Nikki's as long as a responsible adult was there to watch over them during Nikki's recovery. More good news. Dobs was almost trembling with excitement as he stood up and said good bye.

A short while later Andrea was called in to talk to the same caseworker. She was only in the office for a minute or two before she stood up and stormed out, having learned that the children were still to be in Nikki's custody. She fumed as she crossed over the atrium towards the exit, knowing she would have to resort to some other measure to get her daughter back.

While Andrea was storming out of the building, Allison and Jamie were in a large room filled with lots of other kids, some their age, some younger. There was a large television screen in the corner of the room and it was blasting Sesame Street to keep the younger kids entertained. Allison and Jamie sat at the other end of the room waiting to see what would happen next.

Allison was thinking back to the time they were both placed in the same home together for the first time. She was eight years old and Jamie must have been about six. They both started school together at the elementary school in the neighborhood in Mission Viejo where their new foster parents lived. The school was only a few blocks from their home and their new foster Mom walked them to school on their first day and made sure they knew where to go when they got there. That was it. From that point on they were on there own. Their foster mom drove to work every morning before they left for school. She did wake them up and feed them a bowl of cereal before she left for the office. Allison took over the role of mother once she was gone and had Jamie ready for her new first grade class each day. She made sure that her lunch was packed and that she had whatever school supplies she needed.

Allison was in third grade and really liked her teacher. She still remembered Mrs. Kelly. She had taken a special interest in Allison and had made her feel welcome. She even let her stay after school to help out with classroom chores while Jamie sat in the back of the room with a coloring book. It had been a pleasant time for both of the girls, even though it had only lasted a month before their foster mom drank too much one night and went into a blackout and drove off towards San Diego, leaving them both alone in the house. Their stepfather was always out of town on business trips. When the police finally reached him in Dayton, Ohio and told him that his wife had been arrested for vehicular manslaughter in downtown San Diego he told them about the two new foster children that must still be at his home in Mission Viejo. Within hours Allison and Jamie were back in the custody of Child Protective Services and the girls never saw Mrs. Kelly or their new school again.

The next home they were placed in was a family in Dana Point. The home was beautiful and they seemed to be very well off financially. They had a Mexican nanny named Rosa who was always there for them. She lived there, in a little apartment off the side of the garage. The mother and father were seldom home. They hired a piano teacher for the girls who came in twice a week. Allison had just begun to learn a few chords when they were told one evening at dinner by their new foster parents that they would have to be going back to the agency for a while. The foster father was being transferred to Washington D.C. and it just didn't make good sense to take the girls with them. Back to agency housing again, this time for over a year.

That's where Allison met Jeff, a boy from San Diego who had a crush on her. She didn't really feel the same for him but it was kind of nice having her first real boyfriend. Not that they could go anywhere for a date. Except for the occasional field trip to the ballpark or the beach.

On one of these field trips they went to Huntington Beach State Park, right down from the pier at the end of Main Street. She and Jeff had snuck away and walked down to the shops for a while, grabbed a burger and a shake, and then headed back to the State Park end of the beach before they were missed. It had been the closest thing Allison had ever known to a date. A few months later Jeff was taken into a foster home and she never heard from him again.

Allison had been so sure that Nikki would be her new mom. When the police picked her up at the house after school and told her there had been an accident with Nikki, she actually had a difficult time breathing. When they told her they were taking her back to the agency home she looked at Jamie and started to cry. So quickly had everything changed.

Now, as she stared at Jamie who was occupying herself with a puzzle on a small table next to where they sat, she realized they were both probably in for another move. She felt a wave of depression fall over her but tried not to let Jamie know about it. Looking back to the other end of the room towards the television set, she saw Dobs being led into the room by a counselor and she smiled as her sadness slowly lifted.

Once he had them both in the car and was headed back towards the hospital in Newport Beach, he asked them if they wanted to stop and see Nikki before they headed home. Both girls shouted yes as big smiles spread across their faces. Dobs felt better than he had felt all day and thought to himself that things just might work out alright after all.

Allison was sitting in the backseat as they drove down Pacific Coast Highway towards the hospital. She looked out to her right and saw the waves breaking on the beach and in the distance a few ships. Surfers dotted the waves closest to the shore and the sky above the ocean was bright blue with no clouds. She looked at Dobs driving the car and the back of Jamie's head in the passenger seat and felt so very thankful she was where she was.

Once at the hospital, they were told they could only see Nikki for a minute or two. As they walked into her room they both ran up to the bed to hug her, Jamie wrapping her small arms around Nikki's lifeless legs and Allison hugging her neck. Dobs stood and watched the reunion and decided at that moment that as long as Nikki agreed to it, he would stay with her to help out as long as she wanted him to.

He would quit his new job and stay home to care for her. Schwab would take him back later. After all, he controlled his clients. And even so, he was growing bored with the day to day grind. His 401K account had about $500,000 in it so he would just cash it in if need be. Looking at the two young girls hugging Nikki and whispering things back and forth to each other was all he needed to see. He wanted to be a part of all this. He would tell Nikki later when the girls were not around.

"Ok, girls," he said. "Doctor said two minutes and times up. We'll come back tomorrow. Let's go home now." He walked up and kissed Nikki on the forehead to say goodbye. Her eyes told him how much she appreciated what he was doing.

Later that night as he put the girls to bed back at Nikki's house, he decided he would go by his condo the next morning after he dropped them off at school and pick up some clothes and personal items. Then he would come back here and call Morgan at Schwab. Then he would go see Nikki.

He sat at the dining room table and thought about the great change he was about to put himself through. He was walking away from a fairly successful career. But, he knew he wanted to do this more than anything and he was sure Nikki would be happy with the arrangement. A little after nine o'clock he decided to call his daughter Dawn. He wanted to tell her about his plans, wanted to share his excitement with her.

After hearing about what had happened to Nikki and the girls, Dawn told him that what he was doing made her feel so proud of him. She told him if he needed anything at all to just call her. And that she was still waiting to see where they would be stationed, but they should know soon.

CHAPTER 9

For the next two weeks, Dobs supervised the construction of wheelchair ramps for Nikki's house. When she was released she would need it. He paid for it himself and didn't even tell her he was doing it. She found out about it one day when Jamie and Alli were visiting her and Jamie accidentally mentioned it. Nikki smiled and held both of the girls close to her, saying, "We are so lucky to have Dobs around to help."

Every day she asked the nurses when she would be going home. She went to her physical therapy twice a day and did everything they told her to do. Still no real feeling in the legs but she was starting to sense they were her legs again. The therapist said that was a good sign. When she was all alone in her room and had watched all of the TV shows she could stand to watch, she began to think about plans for her future. She would let Paul continue to run the fitness center for her and build an addition in the back for those like herself, who needed special equipment and supervision. She knew that other patients with similar injuries would come to her small facility rather than go to the hospital for therapy. She had it all planned out. It would work.

She even called Paul and told him about her plans. Then she called Dobs and told him. He encouraged her enthusiastically and told her he couldn't wait until she was released. He told her he would be by that evening after dinner for a visit.

When Dobs hit the end button on his cell phone he stared out at the ramp that meandered up towards the front door from the driveway and he smiled with content. She would like it. He stared out at the street from the front door and remembered back to the time they got their first visit from Alli's mother. How Nikki had called the police. How they weren't quite sure what to make of the "crazy bitch" as Nikki preferred to call her.

Would she just give up now and not try to see her daughter again? Not likely, Dobs thought to himself. He turned and walked back towards the kitchen where he began to prepare dinner. The girls were in the back of the house doing homework and had been back there studying quietly since he brought them home from school two hours ago. He turned on the local news as he began to prepare the hamburger patties.

CHAPTER 9

The lead story on Channel Nine news was about a man who had been killed while committing a home invasion in LA. They showed a picture of him and he looked rough. His name was Jake something but Dobs didn't pay much attention to the name. He had been shot when he forced himself into a home. The resident had unloaded all five rounds of his revolver into this Jake character's torso before he had a chance to run away. Apparently the DA was considering charging the shooter since Jake carried no weapon. A small meth lab had also been discovered in one of the spare bedrooms. Dobs knew enough about California gun laws to know that you had to feel threatened by an invader before you could shoot, but he didn't realize the invader had to be armed! What a crock of shit, he thought to himself as he made the patties.

He walked out the side door to light the gas grill and that's when he saw Andrea standing there on the side porch, staring at him with a vacant look in her eye. She looked like she hadn't slept or changed clothes in a while.

"Can I please just see my daughter for a few minutes? Please? I won't try to take her. I just want to see her." Her voice sounded shaky. Dobs pulled his cell phone out of his pocket and started to dial 911. "Please, mister, I won't hurt her. I just want to talk to her."

Dobs closed his flip phone and said, "And then you will leave and never return until the girls are of legal age to decide if they want to see you or not, correct? And then they can come live with you and we can't stop them. And if you break that agreement you will regret it for the rest of your life. Understand?"

"Of course I do. Anything you say. I just need to see Alli." Andrea wore a tan parka and had her left hand in the pocket of the parka the whole time she spoke.

Dobs turned to go back inside, saying, "You wait right here."

When he returned with Alli, Andrea had not moved. But now she reached out with both arms to give Alli a hug and Alli reluctantly hugged her back.

"You've got ten minutes to say what you have to say. Then, like we agreed, you will leave and not try to contact the girls again, at least for a few more years when they can decide for themselves. You've been without Allison for fifteen years so another three years won't make much of a difference. You understand that too, don't you Alli?"

"Sure. I understand. We'll just say goodbye for now." Alli stepped away from her mother as she spoke. "Give us a few minutes."

As Dobs walked back into the kitchen Andrea spoke first. "Now, Alli, listen. We don't have much time. I want you and Jamie to leave with me tomorrow. I have a new house in Phoenix I just bought for the three of us to live in. And a great school for both of you. And I will be there every day for you. I want to …."

"You want to what, Mom. You just told Dobs you would be saying goodbye and when I turn eighteen in a few years we can discuss it. I'm not going anywhere with you right now." Alli was angry, confused with her mother's frantic effort to take her away. "I am happy here, Mom. So is Jamie."

Andrea's tone grew more agitated and rushed. "You're too young to know what you want right now. I am your mother. Doesn't that mean anything at all?"

"Of course it does, but that doesn't mean I want to pack up and leave with you for some place in Arizona."

"But Alli, its such a wonderful high school, Desert Breeze it's called, and its ranked ten out of ten. You just can't get any better than that." Andrea developed a nervous facial tic as she continued. "And we could be such a nice happy family. We could dance. We could do things as a mother and daughter. Don't you see? It will be perfect."

Allison began to realize how unstable her mother really was. She decided to try and calm her by saying, "Mom, its okay. I like the school here and so does Jamie. We can do these mother daughter things in a few more years. Now please, you promised Dobs we would be saying goodbye to each other. So let's just say goodbye and you move on to your new house and we can stay in touch. We can email pictures back and forth. Maybe even get a webcam. How about that, Mom?"

Andrea didn't respond. She just stood there staring at Allison as she put her hands back into the pockets of her parka. When Dobs came back out the side door carrying the plate of burgers, she said, "Okay, Alli. You win, for now. I love you and I will email you when I get settled in?"

"That's great Mom. Thanks." Alli walked over and hugged her mother. As she put her arms around her to squeeze her tight she felt a hard metal object through the thin material of the parka. "Okay, Mom. Time to go."

"Yeah, time to go ma'am." Dobs was putting the burgers on to the grill and Alli was walking towards him, praying inwardly that her mother would just walk away and not try anything else. "Alli, you keep an eye on the burgers while I walk your mother to her car."

Dobs moved towards Andrea and they both walked down the side steps of the porch and headed around towards the front of the house. "You know I didn't park out front?"

"I didn't see you parked out there earlier. Where did you park?"

"Half a block down." Andrea said as they passed under the leaves of a large Eucalyptus tree on the side of the house. "But we can stop right here and say goodbye. And thank you for letting me see her. I am moving to Arizona and I will email her from there, just to stay in touch, if that's okay."

"That will be fine. And again," Dobs turned and looked into her eyes. "Don't come back to this house again."

"Goodbye," she said as she turned to leave. "I won't."

Andrea walked down the block and got into her van. She would just go to Phoenix for now by herself and get things all ready for the girls. She turned on the radio and heard the news about the home invasion shooting. The announcer identified the dead man as Jake Perkins. Andrea was overwhelmed with a sense of relief, followed by sadness. Her brother was dead, but now so was any link to her and what she had paid him to do.

She sat at a red light on PCH and thought about her options. Reaching into the pocket of her parka she took out the gun and put it in her purse, at the same time grabbing her pill bottle and taking another pill. She was beginning to feel a panic attack coming on and needed a Xanax. She headed back to her home in Lake Forest and spent most of the night packing up all of her personal belongings. She would call a mover the next day and schedule a time for them to come pick up her furniture.

Dobs returned to the deck and finished cooking the burgers. He turned off the grill and walked back inside the house to let the girls know it was time to eat. He planned on visiting Nikki by himself tonight, so he could let her know about the visit from Andrea. He told the girls at dinner that he would be back home by nine-thirty, hopefully with some good news about Nikki coming home. He didn't get much of an argument from them when he told them he was going alone. He told them to lock the doors, open them for no one, and to call 911 if Andrea came back. They ate quickly and returned to their bedroom, back into the world of text messaging.

When Dobs got to the hospital he found Nikki sitting up in bed and looking at catalogs of wheelchairs. "So look at this one," she began. "It is motorized but only costs $2,495. What do you think?"

His heart sunk in his chest as he got close enough to see the photo in the catalog with an older woman seated in the chair, cruising down the sidewalk with a big smile on her face. He would call the detective in the morning to see if they had any leads on who had run over Nikki. "Looks okay, I guess. But I might want to get you something a little nicer if that's okay? Any word on your release?"

"Maybe tomorrow! Dr. Muranda is optimistic. It takes a few weeks to actually get the chair you order but he said they give you a nice loaner in the meanwhile."

"Well that's good." Dobs stared down at the catalog and then looked up to Nikki's face. "Allison's mother came by tonight."

"What? That bitch. My God, I can't believe it. Did you call the police?" Nikki was furious.

"I started to, but then she said she only wanted a few minutes to say goodbye. Sounds like she is moving to Arizona, according to Alli. They agreed to stay in touch by email. I told her she could not come back until Alli was eighteen and could decide for herself if she wanted to live with her. She seemed agreeable to that, but she also seemed kind of wigged out."

"What do you mean?"

"You know, kind of drugged up or something."

"That doesn't surprise me." Nikki rolled her eyes.

"But I really think she is leaving and will not be bothering us anymore. As long as we allow her to stay in touch with Alli I think things might be okay. At least I hope so."

"You hope so? Yeah, me too." Nikki turned a page in the catalog. They looked at more wheelchairs and said nothing for a few minutes. Then Dobs reminded her that one of her favorite shows, *The Closer*, was on TV. She put the catalog down and smiled as he turned on the set with her remote.

The next morning Nikki called Dobs and let him know he could come pick her up anytime after noon. The girls were at school and he was putting some finishing touches on the ramp out front. When he was done with the ramp he showered, dressed, and was at the hospital by eleven.

CHAPTER 10

Andrea drove east on Highway 40 in Arizona. The moving truck had left her house in Lake Forest the day before, on a Monday, but they said they wouldn't be in Phoenix until Thursday because they had to pick up two more small moves in San Diego. They told her if she was not in Phoenix when they got there, her stuff would automatically go into storage. She assured them she would be there. She would be staying at a hotel close to her new house and they could reach her on her cell when they were close.

But now as she drove across the desert, it occurred to her that perhaps the best thing to do would be to just let all of her shit go into storage for now. After all, she had lots of time on her hands, now that she had agreed to leave Allison in California for a few more years. If she could take it that is, she thought to herself. She turned the volume up on a Janis Joplin CD she was listening to and cracked her window a bit before she lit a cigarette. She had been driving for three hours and knew she was over halfway to Phoenix.

She decided that since she had the extra time, she would drive all the way across Arizona to see The Painted Desert in the Petrified Forest National Park, one of her favorite places. She found it to be much more beautiful than the Grand Canyon. The sand and rocks were red. It looked like you were on Mars. She loved to just wander the trails there. She had planned on taking Allison and Jamie there but she could just email them some photos.

She thought about her brother, Jake. About how no one would be at his funeral, but that was okay. He deserved to be buried alone. At least he had done one thing for her before he died. Nikki would never hit her again. Andrea only knew what she had seen on the news about Nikki's encounter with Jake's truck, but she knew the damage must have been serious. Too bad she didn't get killed by the truck. That's what Andrea had hoped would happen. But at least she was seriously handicapped. Maybe she would realize the futility of trying to raise the two girls by herself. And even if she got help from that Dobs character, it would hopefully prove to be too much for them and they would have Allison contact her real mother to come and get her.

After passing all exits for Phoenix, Andrea was back in the desert again. She loved driving through the desert. It was October but the temperature was still 105 degrees outside. Her AC worked and the music was playing loud. She was on her meds, heading for The Painted Desert, and feeling good.

Back in Orange County, she knew Allison and Jamie were in school and probably doing just fine. She would send a text to Alli later just to say hello. She looked over at the empty passenger seat next to her and wished Alli was sitting there next to her. But that would all come in time.

When she saw the hitchhiker she knew she would stop and pick him up, as long as he didn't look too creepy. And he didn't. The young man was in his late teens, wore a white t-shirt and jeans and hadn't shaved in a few days. After Andrea stopped he jumped into the passenger seat and threw his small duffle bag into the back of the van.

"Where you headed?" Andrea asked. "And what's your name?"

"Mike. And I'm going to Santa Fe." He seemed like a nice boy.

"Are you in school there?"

"No, I'm taking a year off school for now. Just seeing the countryside." He stared out the window as he spoke.

"I did that when I was about your age. Hitched from LA to Florida."

"Really?" Mike was impressed. "With somebody?"

"Yeah, my best friend Toddster."

"That's a weird name," Mike said.

"Yeah, his name was Todd but he had everyone call him Toddster." Andrea smiled. "He was my first love."

"Yeah, hitchin' is great. I came all the way down from Seattle to LA. Then east to Santa Fe."

"What's in Santa Fe for you?" Andrea asked.

"I am a painter and I hear it's a real cool place for that."

"Really, you're a painter? So am I."

"No shit? What do you paint?" Mike asked.

"Mostly wedding portraits for now, but I've done just about everything." Andrea grew more excited. "I have all of my supplies in the back of the van. Maybe later when we stop I'll get out a sketch pad for you and you can show me what you can do."

"Cool. Are you going all the way to Santa Fe?" Mike asked.

Andrea thought for a moment before answering, realizing she would miss The Painted Desert if she said yes. "Actually, I was going to stop and do some work at The Petrified National Forest. The rocks are actually red there, like on Mars! But I've got some free time, and I haven't seen Santa Fe in years. Sure, why not. We'll go to Santa Fe!"

Just as she said that her cell phone rang. It was Allison. "Heh, Mom. Are you there yet?"

"Oh, hi hon. You mean in Phoenix? No, I am on my way to Santa Fe to do a painting. What's wrong?" Andrea was so happy.

"Nothing, just wanted to call. I thought about our talk and wanted to let you know that I really do appreciate you trying to connect with me. Maybe we can get Nikki and Dobs to let me come visit you at Christmas?"

"Oh that would be wonderful!" Andrea exclaimed, looking over at Mike, who sat there looking out the window at the desert. "But it's going to take some work. So maybe just start by saying little things every now and then about how much you would like to see me. Nikki hates me right now. We need to work on that. Can you do that for me?"

"Sure, she'll come around. I'll just let her know how much it means to me that you are back in my life, even if it's just a little bit for now." Allison sounded so mature. "Well, Mom, I need to go. I will text you my email address and you can send me some pictures when you get back to Phoenix. Okay?"

"Of course, sweetie. I love you, and be good. Bye-bye for now." Andrea hit the end button on her cell and smiled broadly as she told Mike. "That was my daughter. I gave her up for adoption fifteen years ago but I found her and now she is coming back into my life."

"That's wonderful," Mike said. "Where is she?"

"She's in California. She was just adopted by a nice couple and they don't want to let go of her. It's going to be a real battle for me to get her back. But I will get her back."

"So she's fifteen? What's that? Tenth grade?"

"Yes." Andrea smiled and stared straight ahead. "Tenth grade and making very good grades. She has a younger foster sister named Jamie she has been with most of her life, so I will try to get her too."

"Why did you ever give her up in the first place?" Mike asked.

"My life was a mess and I thought she would be better off with a real family that loved her and could provide for her. But I was wrong. She just got moved around a lot in different foster homes. But she still turned out just great." Andrea lit a cigarette and thought back to the depressing time in her life when she told the nurse in the maternity ward to take her baby Allison away and get her a proper home. She was not on any meds yet and her life was a constant whirlwind of ups and downs. She was sure it was for the best. And even today she did not regret her decision. The last fifteen years of her life would not have been a good environment to bring up a daughter. But now, with the meds she was taking, she was ready.

By six that afternoon they were getting close to Santa Fe. They had driven right by the Petrified National Forest exit a few hours earlier and not even considered stopping. Andrea was lost in thought about being with Allison again and she was excited about seeing Santa Fe. Mike had dozed off and was asleep as they approached the exit for Santa Fe. Andrea nudged his knee and he woke up. "Got any special place you want to be dropped off?"

"We're here already? Cool." Mike yawned and stretched his arms. "Yeah, let me call my friend and get his address. You could drop me there if that's okay."

"That's fine. I'll just be checking into a hotel in town." She took the exit and followed the signs for downtown.

Later that evening, after she had dropped Mike off at his friend's house and found a nice hotel, Andrea decided to take in some of the art galleries. She found several on a street very close to her hotel and they were open until nine. The second shop she visited was owned by an older man who sat behind a desk near the rear of the gallery. After looking at most of the paintings, Andrea approached him and handed him her "Artist for Hire" business card.

"So," he began, "you are an artist for hire. As you can see there is no shortage of artists here in Santa Fe." Looking at her card again he saw her California address. "All the way from California?"

"Yeah, actually I am moving to Phoenix. I just came over tonight to check it out. I have heard so much about Santa Fe being a real community of artists."

"That it is," he said, adding, "My name is Walter." He held out his hand to greet her.

"Hi Walter, how are you?" Andrea said as she shook his hand. "I do a lot of wedding portraits and murals."

"That's nice."

"My work is on my website," she said, motioning towards his computer. "Check it out. The address is on the card in your hand." Walter moved over towards the PC and quickly found her website and began looking at her work.

"You are very good, Andrea. Very good." Walter was impressed. He was a few years older than her but she found him to be somewhat attractive.

"Thank you, Walter." She paused. "I am just in town for the evening and I need a good place to eat? Any recommendations?"

"I close up early tonight. Let me take you out to eat some wonderful southwestern cuisine." Walter looked right at her when he spoke but then turned back to her website, adding, "Your work is really quite remarkable."

Andrea decided to have dinner with Walter and spent most of the time telling him about her daughter and some of the time talking about her painting. After dinner, Walter walked her back to her hotel and she invited him up to her room. "Why not have some fun?" she thought to herself, finally letting her mind move away from thinking about her daughter to thinking about how much she wanted to fuck Walter.

After a busy night with Walter he was offering her a position at his gallery. He was a widower and had lost his wife several years ago. She had been his business partner and was also an artist. He wanted Andrea to stay in Santa Fe.

Without any hesitation Andrea let him know that she had no desire to stay in Santa Fe. She had just bought a new house in Phoenix. Perhaps Walter might want to come visit her there on occasion. But no way was she moving to Santa Fe to work in his gallery.

So after a nice breakfast in bed, Andrea said goodbye and Walter returned to work. She checked out of the hotel and was back on the road to Phoenix by ten o'clock. This short trip to Santa Fe had been a good one for her. This time she would definitely make a stop at The Painted Desert. She had promised Alli some pictures and she would not let her down.

CHAPTER 11

Detective Boyle with the Newport Beach Police called Dobs early one morning and asked if he could stop by for a chat. "Of course. We'll be here all day," Dobs said.

He walked out front where Nikki was practicing on the ramps with her new wheelchair – a really cool wheel chair – Dobs had ordered for her. She was getting very good at making the turns that wound down towards the driveway. "Hey," he began, "Guess who's coming to see us this morning?"

"I give up," she replied. "Who?"

"The detective I talked to about Andrea being the one behind your accident."

"Really? He's coming here to talk to us?" Nikki had flown back up the ramp at high speed.

"Be careful on that thing," Dobs told her. "Yeah, he says he has something to talk to us about. Come on in and I'll put on some coffee."

As Dobs cleaned out the coffee carafe over the sink he said, "I still think she had something to do with it." Nikki sat in her chair at the table and flipped through the channels on the remote, not answering him.

When Detective Boyle arrived, Dobs hit the switch on the coffeemaker to brew a new pot he had prepared and they all sat down at the kitchen table. "So how are you feeling?" Boyle asked Nikki.

"I'm slowly coming around. You have some news for us?"

"Well, maybe a lead. He held a manila envelope in his hand and opened it to remove a photograph. He sat it down on the table in front of Nikki. "Have you ever seen this guy before?"

Nikki felt paralyzed all over her body for a second. The photo was a picture of the man that drove the truck into her. "It's him. He was the driver."

"You found him?" Dobs asked the detective.

"He is dead. Died in a shootout last week and when we ran his name we were able to link it up with the lady who was trying to take your kid. This guy was her brother, Jake."

"Wow, that's some amazing police work. And you think she put him up to it?" Dobs asked.

"Yeah, I do. But I can't prove a thing. All I can do is to warn you two about my suspicions and to tell you to be careful. Have you heard from her?"

"She came by last week. Said she was moving to Phoenix and wanted to say goodbye to her daughter. They had a few words and she left. I told her to not come back until her daughter was eighteen in three years and could make her own decisions. She agreed and left."

"Did you tell her she could talk to your daughter in the meanwhile?" Boyle asked.

"Yeah, I said they could email back and forth. After all, it is her real mother, right?" Dobs sighed.

"Dobs, look what she did to me!" Nikki shouted, looking pathetic as she held on to the arms of her wheelchair.

"I know, I know." Dobs paused. "Detective, is there any way we might be able to prove she was behind this?"

"We checked all the cell phone logs and emails from her computer and nothing showed up. She probably knew where he was, went to see him, paid him in cash, and that was it. He was a real low life, a three time loser. And a meth head."

"But she knew where to find him?" Dobs asked.

"Must have." Detective Boyle slid the photo back into the envelope and stood up. "I'm still working a few angles and I will call you as soon as I hear something. Meanwhile, I am going to access your daughter's cell phone records and see what that leads to. At least we will know where Andrea is that way. Thank you both and I will be in touch." He stood up and walked towards the door after shaking hands with Dobs and waving towards Nikki. Then he was gone.

"So," Nikki said.

"What do you mean?" Dobbs asked her.

"The crazy bitch paid her brother to kill me, then, when that didn't work out for her, she came over here and had a chat with you and Allison about her move to Arizona and convinced you both that it would be good to stay in touch?" She was furious.

"Sounds terrible, I know. But we didn't know that when she came over, did we. Now let me work on this. I'll hire an investigator to try and put an evidence trail together for Boyle. Then he can arrest Andrea and we can move forward with our lives. I love you Nikki, you know that."

"I know, and I love you too. But look what she did to me! Please call your guy now." Nikki backed away from the table and headed back out to the ramp in the front yard.

First Dobs called his attorney and got the name and number of his investigator. Scott Fletcher. His lawyer assured him that Scott was the best. Dobs called Scott and explained the situation. After asking lots of questions, Scott told Dobs to relax and wait for him to report back to him after he did some legwork. Dobbs hung up and sat back down at the table with his head in his hands.

After a few minutes he stood up and walked out front. Nikki was on the ramp staring out towards the sky. "He said he would have something for us soon."

She didn't answer at first. Then she said, "I sure hope so, Dobs."

As he watched her practice on the ramps, he remembered how taut and beautiful her legs had been. Now they were emaciating under the sweat pants she always wore. They tried massaging them as the therapist had recommended. They even went to a therapy pool five days a week to try and get them to move. But nothing was working so far. As he watched her try to navigate the ramp, his sadness turned again to anger. He had to find a way to make her better again.

The next day he logged on to the internet early and began searching for treatment centers for paraplegics. He found several and really liked the website for Santa Clara Valley Medical Center. They were working on a new program with Stanford University that involved using cells derived from human embryonic stem cells. And they were having some success.

He called Nikki over to the desk and showed her the site. As they read more about it they became more excited. Then Nikki said, "But if I go up there what will happen to the girls?"

"We'll pull them out of school for a couple of weeks and take them with us," Dobs explained.

"We can't do that." Nikki was somber.

"We could maybe have your aunt come watch them while we are up there? And I could commute back and forth. What do you think? Should I call them?" Dobs said anxiously.

Nikki's face glowed with her excitement. "Yes. But these are clinical trials, right? How can I get accepted? What if it doesn't work?"

Dobs picked up the phone and placed the call. "Let's get some answers."

After a long conversation with one of the staff counselors, Dobs explained to Nikki that the treatment was only successful if performed in the first few weeks after the damage. It had been about two weeks so they would need to move fast. He made an appointment for the next day. Then he turned to Nikki, "Now, here." He handed her the phone. "Call your aunt. What's her name?"

"Aunt Luanne."

"Call Aunt Luanne," Dobs insisted. "Right now."

Nikki maneuvered her wheelchair over to a small cabinet, opened the top drawer, and pulled out her address book. "I think her number is in here. I haven't seen her since Easter. Here it is." Nikki placed the call.

She explained what had happened and the help they needed. She nodded her head up and down as she listened to her aunt's response. Dobs watched nervously trying to guess what was being said. When Nikki finally spoke again she thanked her and said, much to Dobs' relief, "So we will see you about ten in the morning, and you can stay the night for a few nights so the girls can go to school? That's great. Oh thank you so much Luanne. Thank you. Goodbye."

Dobs wanted to pick Nikki up out of her chair and dance around the room with her. "Oh my God, Nikki. This is such good news."

Nikki hugged him as she said. "And the girls should be just fine too. And you can come back here and take care of them this weekend when Luanne goes back to Riverside. But she can come back again next week if we need her."

"Let's pack your suitcase." Dobbs moved towards the bedroom. "I'll get it."

Nikki watched as he left the room and closed her eyes, saying a prayer to thank God that she had Dobs to help her get through this. When he walked back in carrying the small suitcase she smiled up at him through tears of happiness.

When Dobs picked the girls up at school that afternoon he explained it all to them. They both remembered Luanne from her visit on Easter. They both liked her so there was no problem at all, which caused Dobs to also utter a “Thank God” under his breath.

The next day Luanne arrived at nine thirty and they were on the road by ten. The drive to San Jose was about six hours and their appointment was at four o clock. So there would be no time to stop for lunch. Nikki’s catheter would be adequate if she needed to go and Dobs would make a very quick stop only if he needed to. Dobs had made sandwiches for the trip and a thermos of iced tea. Once they got over to the 5 he knew he could go fast. Just getting there was the issue. It would take too much time with any bad traffic. So he decided on the 405 to the 101. In six hours they were pulling into the Valley Medical Center.

Dobs had copies of all of her records form Hoag Hospital and the check-in went very quickly. He signed everything as the responsible party in case her insurance did not cover it and by four thirty they were in her private room, looking out the window at Silicon Valley, waiting for a doctor to show up.

Dr. Becker, a female physician in her thirties, introduced herself when she came in about five o’clock and answered all of their questions. Nikki would be in the center for at least two weeks. They would do some initial analysis tomorrow and then shoot for a procedure date before the weekend. She let them know the risks of the procedure up front. Not only would it maybe not work at all, it might make future rehabilitation even more difficult. Nikki did not hesitate to sign the release paperwork and the doctor left them alone in the room at five thirty.

"So, I guess I need to find a hotel," Dobs said.

"Unless you want to sleep here with me. The nurse said that sofa over there folds out into a bed."

"Really?" Dobs walked over to the sofa and tried to figure out how it worked. He pulled the top cushion off, released a small latch, and the bottom of the sofa pulled out about two more feet, morphing into a twin sized bed. "Wow, I am impressed. I'm here for the night, like it or not."

Nikki was looking at the menu. "Take a look at this, Dobs. They have quite a menu."

"Really?" He walked over and looked over her shoulder at it. "I'll take the Shrimp Scampi."

"And I will go with the Fettuccini Alfredo. I can't believe this menu. Hope it's good." Nikki's spirits were the highest they had been since before she got hurt.

They ate dinner, and it was very good. Then they watched a few shows on TV before going to sleep about ten o'clock. Nikki called the girls before going to sleep and said goodnight, relieved to hear that all was well with Aunt Luanne. Throughout the night the nurses came by to check Nikki's vitals and Dobs slept through it all without waking up.

In the morning, the first question Nikki had was where do they get the embryo cells. "This stem cell stuff,

I thought that was illegal?" she asked Dr. Becker during her morning consult.

"The stem cells are derived from a single embryo that was created through in vitro fertilization. The patients sign an informed consent allowing the cells to be used for research. All perfectly legal, not to worry. The FDA approved the procedure for clinical trials in 2009." Dr. Becker spoke with confidence, her long auburn hair pulled back into a bun on top of her head.

"Really?" chimed in Dobs. "And it works?"

"We don't expect complete recovery but we do expect some dramatic improvements. We will do the procedure tomorrow morning, after a few more tests today. Once you are in recovery, you will need to stay here for a while for the rehabilitation therapy."

"How long?" Nikki asked, thinking about the girls.

"Maybe three weeks, maybe six. We will see." Dr. Becker looked down at her chart. "I will see you in the morning. Not to worry, this is a simple procedure." She turned and walked out.

"Wow," said Nikki. "I can't believe you found this place!"

"Yeah, I know." Dobs held her hand with one hand and a menu in his other, saying, "Do you get to order breakfast? The menu is amazing." Everything from bagels to crepes was on the menu, like it would be at an elegant resort. Nikki chose a bowl of fruit and Dobs ordered French Toast and sausage.

After eating, the rest of the day consisted of more tests. Nikki called Luanne and everything was fine. The girls were in school and she would be picking them up at three o'clock. She told Luanne that Dobs would be driving back late Friday night so she could go back to Riverside for the weekend.

Just before they were ready to order dinner, Nikki was told she needed a special diet to prep for her procedure in the morning. Dobbs was looking over the menu, trying to decide between the burger or the steak when his cell phone rang.

It was Scott, the investigator. He had a lead he was working on about Andrea and her brother Jake. Apparently Andrea had visited a bar in San Pedro a while back asking about her brother's whereabouts. The bartender had remembered her and told Scott she left that day without finding her brother. But he had given Andrea's business card to him the next time he came into the bar. That was it. But it was certainly a lead of some sort. She had been trying to contact him, maybe to see if he would help her hurt Nikki. But, unfortunately according to Scott, the trail died there. Jake had no cell phone records since he had used a throwaway phone for years. And even if they could subpoena Andrea's phone records they could only tell that she had received a call from someone in San Pedro, with no ID on the caller available. It sounded like a dead end to Dobs too. He thanked Scott and ended the call.

"That was the PI." He looked at Nikki. "No solid connection, but she did communicate with her brother before you got hurt but there is no trail to prove it. He said he would keep working on it. But I'm still going to let Detective Boyle know what he found out. Maybe he can question her again."

"Terrific." Nikki did not seem surprised. "Do you really think she paid to have me killed? Just to get Alli?"

"I think so, and so does Scott. I even think Detective Boyle suspects it. But there is no way to prove it. Her brother is dead and so all she has to do is deny it. No other parties involved."

"Unless," Nikki offered.

"Unless what?" Dobs asked.

"Unless we can trick her into admitting it somehow. Have her put away for a long time."

"And how would we do that?" Dobs sounded dubious.

"Well, what if I were to call her up and invite her to come and visit Allison. We could even have her stay at the house. Then you and I could wear a wire and record us all as we told her we will let her have Allison as long as she admits to some involvement with what happened to me. You know. Tell her the police showed me a picture of her brother and I had identified him as the driver. Tell her they could not prove she had anything to do with it. And that if she told us that she had her brother run into me because she was so desperate to get her daughter, that we truly understood how much she must love Allison." Nikki paused to catch her breath and take a drink of water. "I mean, we know she is half crazy, right? She may just open up and admit everything if she thinks I am willing to let her have Allison. Hell, we'll tell her she has to take Jamie too."

"Doesn't sound very realistic to me." Dobs despaired.

"Yeah, but you're not the nutcase. She is. I think she might go along with it. Especially if she believed the police had no proof that she was involved at all. We could even have Detective Boyle call her and tell her he could not connect her at all with her brother's actions."

A nurse walked into the room to take her vitals. Still facing Dobs, Nikki said, "Just think about it, Dobs. It might be the best plan."

"I'll think about it. Now you just slow down and relax while she takes your vital signs. You've got a big day tomorrow. I've been doing some research. Did you know that these stem cells create a sort of sheath that allows the transmission of electrical signals along the spinal cord that triggers muscles to move? They will be injecting about two million cells into your spinal cord in the morning. That ought to get something going! Don't you think?" Dobs was trying to be playful.

"Let's hope so," said Nikki as the nurse took her blood pressure. "Where did you get that information anyway?"

Dobs held up a small brochure he had been looking at. "It's all in here." He handed the brochure to Nikki, who shook her head no.

"Don't need it. I have faith. Anyway, I want my dinner. I think I get Jell-O and broth. Yum. What are you going to order?"

"I'm going with the steak." Dobs was still amazed at the menu selection the hospital offered and very grateful for it.

CHAPTER 12

Andrea was arranging furniture and hanging pictures in her new house in Phoenix when her cell phone rang. "Hello?"

"Hello, is this Andrea Perkins?" Boyle asked.

"Yes, who is this?"

"This is Detective Boyle in Newport Beach. We spoke a few weeks back about the incident where the woman got hit on PCH."

"Yes?" Andrea froze.

"I have some more questions if that's okay. Do you have a few minutes?"

"Sure."

"We just got some information that indicates you were in San Pedro looking for your brother some time before the incident, is that correct?"

"Well, yes. I was looking for him. But I never found him. And now he is dead and probably a lot better off than he was alive."

"Why do you say that, ma'am?" Boyle was surprised at her response.

"Because he had such a miserable life, that's why." Andrea wanted to hang up. "Is there anything else, Detective?"

"Could I get an address for you? Just in case we need to contact you again."

Reluctantly she gave him her new address, regretting it as soon as she did. He thanked her and said goodbye. Andrea stood and stretched as she looked around her new living room. Her bright colored artwork covered the walls. She picked up her hammer and headed down the hall towards what would soon be Allison's bedroom.

She carefully placed a tarp down to cover the carpet before she opened the fresh can of rose colored paint she had chosen for Alli's walls. She began talking to herself under her breath, even though she was alone, saying, "Why the fuck did I give him my address? I mean, how stupid of me. But, then again, they have nothing on me so what difference does it make. Now, if Jake hadn't gotten himself shot, that would be bad. But there was no other connection. So, I'll be fine." Once she was finished she decided to go out for a drive while the paint dried. She needed some air.

CHAPTER 12

The following week a summons arrived in her mailbox from the Orange County Superior Court. They were notifying her of a deposition she was being asked to give regarding the attempted murder of Nikki Pittilon of Laguna Beach. For her convenience the deposition would take place by proxy in the Mesa County Courthouse in Phoenix the following Tuesday morning. She could appear by herself or with counsel.

"Fuck." Andrea threw the summons on to the kitchen table. Things had been going so well for her. The house was coming together nicely and was all ready for Allison.

She walked into the kitchen and just stood there looking at the walls adorned with small curios and pictures she had put up earlier. Lace curtains with small yellow flowers hung over the kitchen window above the sink. Outside the window she could see the sand in her backyard. Although the large cactus garden was lovely, she missed having a lawn already. Large round stones were interspersed around the yard in an asymmetrical formation. Her own little mini Stonehenge she thought to herself as she laughed. Had she forgotten to take her pill?

She walked over to the island in the middle of the kitchen and looked at the pill bottles resting in the center of the tile surface. She looked at a small notepad she kept next to the pills and saw that she had taken her pills earlier. She decided to pour herself a glass of Chardonnay and take it out to the back patio where she had her easel set up underneath a nice awning that blocked most of the sun. She would continue working on her new painting until it was dinnertime. It was a brightly colored picture of Allison.

As she looked into the eyes of the picture she was painting, she felt the effects of the Chardonnay as she grew melancholy thinking about all of the years she had missed watching Allison grow into the fine young woman that was staring back at her from the portrait. She knew nothing about her kindergarten years, the time she spent in elementary school, and only a few random pieces of information Allison had told her about middle school. 'Wouldn't it be wonderful if she could have the high school years with Allison?' she thought to herself as she went inside to quickly pour another glass of wine.

Once back at the easel with her wineglass in one hand and the brush in the other, she began to grow inspired, quickly adding long stokes of blonde and brown as she colored Alli's hair. Staring into the eyes again she became overwhelmed with the thought that she must find a way to get Allison now. Not wait three years. Now, she thought to herself as she set the wineglass down on the table and picked up her cell phone.

Allison had just gotten home from school. Aunt Luanne had picked her up after also picking up Jamie at the middle school a few blocks down Park Avenue from Laguna Beach High School, where Allison was now a freshman. She saw the call was from her mother so she walked out into the side yard to answer it. "Hello, Mom."

"Oh Allison, I miss you so much."

"How you doin' Mom?" Allison asked nervously.

"Oh, Allison, I am so wonderful. The house is so beautiful. I am out on the patio painting a picture of you." The wine mixed with her meds always surprised her, even though she had been told not to mix the two.

CHAPTER 12

"I just wanted to call and see how you are doing. I know you just started high school there. Do you like it?"

"Its alright I guess. I don't know that many people."

"And how is your foster mom doing?"

"She is up in San Jose getting therapy. Dobs and Aunt Luanne are taking care of us while she is gone." Allison played with the leaves of an avocado tree while she talked.

"How long is she gone for?" Andrea's interest had suddenly increased.

"Not sure, maybe a month or so. But they think this new treatment can help her walk again, so it's worth it for sure."

"Of course it is, Alli. So, what do you think about a quick little visit over to see me some time soon while she's gone?"

"I don't think Dobs will go for it, but I could ask. You mean like for weekend or something, right?"

"Right, a weekend." Andrea held her breath.

"He may say okay since he has to drive back here from San Jose each weekend since Luanne can't stay over. I can ask." Allison looked upon the whole idea as an adventure, as would most teenagers.

"When can you talk to him sweetie?" Andrea was buzzing at this point.

"I can ask him tonight when he calls. And then I can call you tomorrow."

"No, call me back tonight as soon as you talk to him, okay?"

"Okay, Mom. I will. I'll call you later, probably about eight thirty."

"Thanks sweetie. Talk to you then. Bye for now."

"Oh Mom?"

"Yes?"

"You mean me and Jamie, right. Not just me."

"Of course I mean both of you."

"Because that's probably the only way he would say okay to it. So he could stay in San Jose all weekend with Nikki."

"Of course, tell him I will buy round trip tickets for next Friday afternoon and you can get your Aunt to drop you off at John Wayne Airport. Can she pick you up on Sunday night?

"I can ask," Allison said. "I'll call you tonight, Mom."

After Andrea hung up she felt like she was walking on the clouds. She began waltzing around the deck, pirouetting in large circular patterns as she stopped every few seconds to look out at her miniature Stonehenge rocks and the cactus garden. The sun was beginning to go down and the sky was turning a bright rose color. Andrea immediately connected this color in the sky with the rose color of the paint she had used in Allison's bedroom and interpreted the event as a sign that everything was going to work out just fine.

That evening Allison called her back and said that Dobs told her he would think about letting her come for a weekend but he wanted to talk with Nikki first, after she had a few days to recover from her procedure.

The following Tuesday morning Andrea parked her van in the courthouse parking lot and found her way to the room where she was supposed to give her deposition. She walked in and the receptionist told her to have a seat while she waited. After a few minutes a woman in her late twenties walked out of one of the office doors, walked up to her with her hand held out, and introduced herself as Jane Smalley. The card she handed Andrea had a title under her name of Assistant Prosecutor for Mesa County. She seemed friendly enough as she escorted Andrea into her office and sat down at a rectangular table across from where she asked Andrea to sit. She placed a file folder down on the table in front of her and smiled as she said, "I have been asked by the District Attorney's office in Orange County California to ask you some questions." She set a small tape recorder down on the table. "Your answers will be recorded and transcribed and then sent back to them. I see you have chosen not to have an attorney present?"

"I really don't need an attorney," Andrea answered her. "I haven't done anything wrong." She was so glad she had taken an extra Xanax before leaving home. She was settling into a nice groove to answer questions and get this whole thing out of the way as quickly as possible.

Jane Smalley stared across the table at Andrea and asked her the first question. "Ms. Perkins, is Perkins your legal last name?"

"Yes."

She then asked her to verify her present address and former address, before she asked, "You were never married?"

"Yes, years ago, but I took my name back after the divorce."

"And was your brother's name Jake Perkins?"

"Yes."

"When was the last time you spoke with your brother?"

"It's been over a year." Andrea knew she was now committing perjury. But she remained calm.

"Did you attempt to contact him last month in San Pedro?"

"Yes, I left my card with a bartender down there but never heard from him."

"What phone number is on your business card?"

"My cell phone number. The one with my California area code. But I'm having it changed to an Arizona number soon. I live here now so I might as well have a local number." Andrea chuckled nervously.

"And your brother never called you on your cell phone last month?"

"No."

"The records from the cell phone have several calls on them from pay phones in the Long Beach area."

"Those were probably just inquires about my work. I do have a website advertising my artwork and I get calls just about every day."

"From pay phones?" Smalley looked directly at her.

"I don't ever know what kind of phone they are calling from."

"But if they were looking at your website to get your phone number, why would they be calling you from a pay phone. Wouldn't they most likely have access to a cell phone or landline?"

"I don't know. What difference does it make?" Andrea crossed her legs.

CHAPTER 12

"Well, is it possible that one of these calls was from your brother, Jake? And you arranged to have him try to kill Nikki Pittilon by running her over with his truck?"

"That's absurd." Andrea uncrossed her legs and put both elbows on the table. "I never talked to my brother. I would suggest you ask him but he's dead. Got shot breaking into someone's house."

"Yes I know, Ms. Perkins. Did you attend his funeral?"

"No, I didn't even know about it until he was already in the ground."

"Doesn't sound like you are very upset that he is dead, are you?"

"Not really. Jake was a tortured soul, always had been. A very bad man. I stayed away from him. We were not close at all, even as children." Andrea paused. "Ms. Smalley, I'm curious. Why do you think Jake had anything to do with Ms. Pittilon's accident?"

"Because Nikki Pittilon identified your brother Jake as the driver of the truck that hit her. Do you know Ms. Pittilon?"

"Yes, I know her." Andrea felt like the Xanax was wearing off and she was starting to wish she had brought an attorney with her.

"She is the foster mother to my daughter, Allison. I've seen her recently. I was trying to see if she will let me have my daughter back."

"And what did she say?"

"She said no. At least no for now. But when Allison turns eighteen she can come live with me and that's only a few years away."

"You gave up Allison for adoption when she was born, correct?"

"Correct, I wasn't ready to be a mother."

"And you haven't seen or talked to her in fifteen years, correct?"

"Not until just recently. I took her up to meet my folks in Santa Cruz."

"With Ms. Pittilon's permission?"

"Of course."

"And how did that visit go."

"It was cut short. Alli didn't feel well and called Ms. Pittilon to come pick her up." Andrea held back on saying anything about Grandpa. "But I think they are going to let her come visit me here in Arizona for Christmas this year."

"Really?" Jane Smalley paused and looked through the file. "That's interesting."

"Well, I don't know for sure but I should find out soon." Andrea crossed her legs again and kicked her leg nervously. "Are we just about done here?"

"Yes, I think we are done for now. I will forward your answers to Orange County and they can contact you if they have any more questions." Jane Smalley stood up. "Thank you for your time, Ms. Perkins."

Andrea stood up and said goodbye as they shook hands. Once outside of the building she lit a cigarette. Looking around she saw several other nervous looking people also smoking cigarettes. "Thank God this is over," she thought to herself as she walked quickly towards the parking garage.

CHAPTER 13

Dobbs was driving home from San Jose on Friday afternoon. The last two weeks had gone well for Nikki. Her procedure had been successful and she had begun some intensive therapy. He wished he could have stayed for the weekend but he had to go home and take care of the girls. He had to break it to Allison that Nikki had said no way about the visit to see her Mom. He would be back in San Jose on Monday.

With all of the free time he recently had on his hands while Nikki was undergoing her therapy, he had begun to think about writing a screenplay again. He had a great story idea about a stockbroker who had embezzled most of his client's money over a period of years and almost got caught. But he had masterfully covered his trail in fake trades so it looked like nothing had been done wrong if anyone ever looked at his client's accounts. Since the terrible sell off that began in 2008 up until the recovery in 2010, more people had become aware of the dangers of the market. He thought a good story about a dishonest broker should do real well. Of course, he would have to add some love and sex into the story.

As he got closer to Los Angeles he began to think that he may not have it in him anymore. After all, it had been a long time. But, he could give it a try. If he didn't go back to work for awhile he would have plenty of time to work on it. Too bad he didn't have any good connections in Hollywood. He would have to find an agent to represent him, and he was a nobody in the business. Oh well, it would give him something to work on for now while he took care of Nikki.

He called his daughter, Dawn, and gave her an update on what was happening. He asked her about her wedding plans with Tim.

"Well, things have changed a bit," Dawn told him.

"Wedding is off?" Dobs asked.

"Not exactly. We're still getting married. But not for a while. I think I should finish college first and Tim agrees. After all, they might end up sending him overseas and it would just be better if we waited."

"But you guys are still good, right?"

"Oh yeah. We're real good. How about you and Nikki?"

"You know I quit my job to take care of her for awhile."

"Yeah, you told me that. Are you living at her place?"

"Only on the weekends. She's in a medical center up in San Jose getting treatment. I stay up there with her all week and come home to watch the girls on the weekends."

"That's nice."

"Yeah, Nikki's aunt takes care of them during the week, which is great."

"Dad?"

"Yeah."

"You think you and Nikki might get married?"

Dobs hesitated. "Well, I would love to marry her. I'm just not sure that now's the time to bring it up since she is so focused on her rehab. Know what I mean?"

"Dad, if you think she loves you it's okay to bring it up, trust me." Dawn assured him.

"Well, I'll see how it goes. Anyway, I love you. Want to come for dinner tomorrow night?"

"Sure, Tim's at Pendleton and my calendar is wide open."

"Just come by Nikki's place tomorrow afternoon. Maybe I'll cook on the grill." Dawn loved his barbeque chicken. He gave her the address before they said good-bye to each other. It would be nice to see her and let her get to know the girls a little better.

Once he got home and greeted Luanne and the girls at the door, he realized how tired he was. He helped Luanne carry her suitcase to the car and thanked her for all of her help. She told him she would be back Sunday afternoon about four o'clock and he told her that would be great.

Then he walked back inside and sat down at the kitchen table with Allison and Jamie. He ordered pizza and cinnamon sticks from Pizza Hut, which made Alli and Jamie very happy. Then he asked them to both sit down at the table for a few minutes, where he explained to them that Nikki did not want them to go visit Andrea at all. At least not until they were older. Her recovery was a number one priority and she did not feel comfortable letting the girls run off to Arizona anytime soon.

Allison took it pretty well. Jamie acted like she didn't really care one way or the other as she said, "Call us when the pizza gets here?" She got up and ran back to her room, leaving Alli and Dobs alone at the table.

"I guess it's for the best. I mean I want to see her but I understand this might not be the best time for it. I'll call her and let her know. But thanks for asking, Dobs." Alli kissed him on the forehead and slowly walked back to her room. Dobs sat in silence waiting for the pizza, hoping things would go well for Allison when she called Andrea with the news that she would not be coming to see her.

Andrea answered her cell phone as she was pulling into her driveway. After a moment of stunned silence, she responded to Alli. "She said there was no way you could come?"

"Yeah, pretty much. She said I needed to wait until I was eighteen. But maybe one day she will change her mind but for now it's a no." Allison didn't seem to be as upset about it as Andrea expected her to be.

"Well, that's just much to long to wait." She paused, thinking. "Listen, I may come and get you anyway. Would that be okay with you?"

"Doesn't sound like a great idea, Mom. They'll probably call the cops on you."

"Maybe, but I want to see you and I am your mother so that should count for something with the police, if they do call them."

"Well if you come you better do it during the week when Dobs is not around. But I still think it's a real bad idea. Can't you just wait a while until Nikki gets better?"

"Maybe, we'll see. But I'll just be coming for you if I do come, you understand that, right? Jamie is too young and she's not really mine, like you are."

"I understand, Mom. But please just wait a few weeks at least. Can't you do that?"

"We'll see. But I am very disappointed in that Nikki. I just don't see what harm it would do for you to be able to come visit your mother. I'll call you when I figure this whole thing out. Goodnight sweetie. Oh, one more thing. Write down my email address so you can reach me that way if you need to. It is ARTISTFORHIRE@AOL.COM".

"Got it Mom. So goodnight. I love you." Allison hung up. Her Mom was acting crazy, but she was still her mother. Allison climbed under her covers and thought about what it might be like actually living with her as mother and daughter. She looked across the room at Jamie sitting at the computer desk chatting with a new friend on Facebook and knew she would not be able to come with her. She had known Jamie most of her life. She was her younger sister and she loved her. How could she just abandon her now, even though Nikki and Dobs would take good care of her?

Allison closed her eyes and tried to imagine what it might be like in Phoenix. She could go to Dobs and explain to him that she really wanted to go see her, maybe even move there permanently. Ask him what he really thought about it. But, if she did, he would go to Nikki and it would quickly be over. Allison knew she had to decide by herself. She just wished she knew her Mom better, knew that she was not going to act so crazy all the time. Allison fell asleep thinking about it and slept soundly through the night.

The next morning Dobs told the girls that his daughter Dawn was coming for dinner that afternoon. They had met Dawn once or twice and really liked her a lot, so they were both excited about it. Jamie asked Dobs if her new friend, Sara, could sleep over and he said okay. He wanted the girls to have good, solid friendships now that they were all going to be one big family. He even asked Allison if there was anyone she wanted to have over for the night but she couldn't think of anyone she wanted to invite.

Late in the evening, after Dawn had gone home and Jamie and Sara had set up their sleepover in the living room, Allison was back in her bed under the covers, once again thinking about her mother. After she had been asleep for a few hours she was awakened by a soft, firm hand covering her mouth. It was Andrea. She had noiselessly crawled in through the bedroom window. She told Allison to be very quiet as she helped her pack her things. Allison wanted to say goodbye to Jamie but knew she couldn't. Andrea told her she could call her the next day to say goodbye.

CHAPTER 13

"Mom, I don't think this is a real good idea."

"Just leave that up to me. Now, hush. And pack your bag." Andrea stood over her and Allison felt compelled to do as she was told.

The next morning Dobs was in the kitchen making pancakes. When Jamie came in with Sara he told them they could go wake up Allison. When they came back and told him she wasn't there, he rushed to the bedroom to see for himself. There was no note. The window was cracked open a bit and the room looked emptier than it usually did. The closet door was open and most of her clothes were gone. Dobs sat down on the edge of the bed and covered his face with his hands while Jamie and Sara stood in the doorway watching him. He knew what had happened and he knew he had to call the police. He walked back in the kitchen and picked up his cell phone, noticing there was a text from Allison. "i'm fine, dobs. just want to spend a little time with my mom. please don't worry about me. And tell jamie i love her and will call her later."

CHAPTER 14

Andrea had been driving for about eight hours while Allison slept in the passenger seat. When she awoke, the sun was coming up and there were mountains along the horizon outside her window. "Are we in Arizona?"

Andrea stared straight ahead. "No, sweetie. We're not going to Arizona yet."

"But your new house there?" Allison exclaimed.

"Yeah, well, we can't go there for now. Your mother will have the police and the FBI looking for us and that's the first place they will look." Andrea reached into her purse and pulled out a small black throwaway cell phone and held it out for Allison. "Here is your new phone."

"But I have a phone." Allison reached into her purse to find her phone but it was gone. "It's not here."

"I threw it out last night. That's the first way they could track us. Here, take your new phone."

"But I really liked my old phone." Allison took the small black flip phone and opened it up. "And I had all my numbers in it."

"That's okay. You only need a few numbers for now. And you know the important ones, correct?"

"Yeah, I guess so." Allison paused. "So where are we going?" She felt a wave of fear come over her.

"To a friend's place for now up in Spokane, Washington. Then we'll see from there. The important thing is that we are together at last." Andrea looked at Allison smiling. Her tired eyes were bloodshot, either from crying or just lack of sleep.

"I'm hungry," Allison said as she looked out her window towards the mountains.

"I saw a sign for a truck stop restaurant coming up in a few minutes. They always have good food, you know."

Allison didn't know anything about truck stops. "Sure, sounds good, Mom." She adjusted her ipod to a louder volume for Fleetwood Mac and closed her eyes. "Let me know when we get there."

Allison drifted off into a half sleep and Andrea kept staring straight ahead until she finally saw the sign for the restaurant. Allison woke up as they were pulling into the truck stop. She saw long lines of huge trucks parked symmetrically along the front of the parking lot. "Why are they all parked like that?"

"They're catching some zzz's," Andrea answered. "I can't wait to taste this breakfast. Come on, let's go."

CHAPTER 14

They walked through a large gift shop on the way to the restrooms. Allison stopped and looked at a few small gifts she thought about buying for Jamie. Andrea turned around and waved her arm for her to follow her. "You must stay with me. We can look at that stuff later."

After the restroom, they entered the restaurant and had an amazing breakfast of pancakes, eggs, hash browns, and bacon. They were both so hungry that very little was said while they ate. Andrea wiped her mouth and said, "Your turn to drive. That's okay, right?"

"Sure, I can drive. Just tell me which way to go." She was still finishing her pancakes.

"We'll just stay on Interstate 5 the rest of the day, then I'll take over for the final leg." Andrea took a sip of coffee and smiled. "Unless you want to line up out there with those big rigs and catch some shuteye?"

"No, that's okay. I'll drive." Andrea was freaking her out a little.

Once back on the road heading north, Andrea fell asleep and Allison adjusted her ipod volume as she drove the van, mostly staying in the far right lane. She knew Spokane was somewhere up in Washington. But they were still in California, soon to be entering Oregon. Allison had instructed her to wake her up when she was hungry for some lunch.

Andrea looked over at her mother asleep in the passenger seat and thought about what it might be like living with a real mom, someone who shared the same genetic makeup, someone who could give her unconditional love. She smiled and felt most of her fears subside. For the first time today she was happy to be alive and happy to be with her mother.

After only a few hours sleep, Andrea jerked and bolted upright from her sleeping position. It happened so fast it startled Allison and she almost lost control of the vehicle. "What are you doing, Mom?"

"Oh," Andrea began, "this always happens when I forget to take my meds. It just jerks me out of a deep sleep so fast. Scares me sometimes too. Sorry about that."

"What medicines?" Allison asked.

"For my bipolar disorder."

"What's that?" Allison had heard of it before but wanted to ask about it.

"It makes me go up and down all the time. God, I hope you don't get it too. It really sucks. But, the meds do really help." Andrea put the pills in her mouth and swallowed them down with a half empty water bottle that was in the cup holder. "If I don't take these pills anything goes!"

"Well I'll try to make sure you always take them," Allison offered.

"But, sometimes, I still like to have a little fun. Say, what do you say we see if there's a concert you might want to see in Portland tonight."

"Maybe we should talk about it after your meds kick in," Allison said, sounding like the mother.

"Maybe so. Hey, let's get off here and go to McDonalds for lunch." The highway sign indicated it was one of several choices for them at the next exit. "I do think we might make Portland by tonight. It is a very cool place. It's a real magnet for runaway teens so probably not a good place for us to live."

The phrase 'runaway teens' raced through Allison's mind as she wondered what that would be like. To be a teenager and to run away from your parents. She couldn't understand it. Maybe if they were abused, she could see that. But just to run away because they didn't agree with what their parents wanted them to do? Made no sense. They should spend some time in one of the agency homes she had been in and see how they liked those rules. "I don't get the runaway thing," she said out loud.

"Well lots of kids do it. I did it, you know. I only went away for a few days but it really scared my parents. I got picked up in San Francisco and they had to drive up and get me. And they were pissed."

"Oh well, I just don't get it." Allison put her turn signal on for the exit ramp. "If they have a home and parents who love them they ought to stay there. At least that's how I see it." Allison began to think of Dobs and Nikki. Although they weren't her actual parents, she knew they loved her and it occurred to her that she was actually running away from them. Confusion swept through her mind as she looked at her mother, who was lacing up her shoe laces for lunch at McDonalds. Allison decided she would call Jamie from the restroom when they got there, maybe even say hello to Dobs.

Andrea ordered a salad, fries, and coffee while Allison ordered a Big Mac combo meal. They sat down at a small plastic table overlooking the parking area and a gas station.

"Got to get gas when we leave," said Andrea with a mouthful of salad.

"Right." Allison nodded her head in agreement.

After they had both quickly devoured their meals, Allison got up to use the restroom and picked up her purse to take with her. Andrea grabbed her hand. "No phone calls yet, sweetie. Wait until we get to where we're going. Here, I'll hold your purse."

Allison quickly used the restroom and returned to the table. "Mom?"

"Yes?" Andrea had a huge smile on her face. She was looking at a Portland newspaper, the entertainment section, and she announced, "You like Black Eyed Peas, correct?"

"Yeah, sure. But I don't want to go to a concert tonight. Let's just get to where we're going." Allison grabbed her purse and stood there waiting.

Andrea stood up and they both walked out. Andrea lit a cigarette as soon as they hit the fresh air and said, "My turn to drive."

Allison handed her the keys and said, "Don't forget to get gas."

"Thanks sweetie, I just might have forgotten!" Andrea started the car and drove it over to the gas pumps across the parking lot.

Once back on the interstate, Allison asked a question she had wanted to ask for a while. "Mom, where is my father?"

"Oh dear, I suppose I should let you know a little more about what's going on. You'll be meeting your real father tomorrow when we get to Spokane. He lives there.

I haven't seen him in years but I called him and he said he can't wait to see us."

"What does he do? What is he like?" Allison asked. "Was he there when you gave me up?"

"No, he wasn't around, or I might have kept you. He's a writer. A science fiction writer."

"Really?"

"Well, he used to be pretty successful at it. I haven't seen him in long time." Andrea had a dreamy look on her face.

"And he wants to see me, right?" Allison asked.

"Correct."

"And does he know that you kind of kidnapped me?" Allison said this softly. "Even though I went along with it of course."

"He knows."

"That's good. What's he like?"

"He told me he still writes and has several books published. But he also told me that we must accept him for who he is when we see him."

"What does that mean?"

"Well," Andrea began to explain. "He has become a nudist and doesn't like to wear clothes anymore."

"What? You're kidding! That's great. Maybe I can have another Grandpa moment but with my real Dad this time." Allison was pissed. "Why do we need to go see him?"

"Relax, sweetie. He said he would wear clothes while we are visiting him. It's not like he's always nude."

"Well, that's comforting. God, Mom, this is crazy. Isn't there somewhere else we can go? What about the Phoenix house you told me about."

"Can't go there until you are officially mine. And that's a long ways off right now if Nikki decides to press charges against me for taking you."

"Maybe I could talk to her. Let her know that I really want to go with you?"

"Maybe, hearing it from you might be better than whatever Dobs told her. We can call her right now using one of these throwaway phones, if you're up to it?"

"I don't have the number for the hospital she's at. Somewhere in Sunnyvale. But I can ask Dobs for it tonight."

"Okay, we can stop for dinner in Portland. You can call from there." Andrea kept her eyes straight ahead on the highway.

CHAPTER 15

Dobs was sitting at the kitchen table on Sunday afternoon talking to Detective Boyle when he heard Jamie's phone ring in the distance. "That might be her calling," he said to Boyle. They both slowly stood up and quietly walked back towards Jamie's room.

"If that's Allison let me talk to her," Dobs said as he walked in. Jamie nervously handed her phone to him. Dobs began, "Allison, where are you? Are you okay?"

"I'm fine. I want to call Nikki. Can you give me her number at the hospital?" Allison sounded fine. "I'm sorry to put you through all of this but I really want to spend some time with my Mom."

"Allison, is she right there with you?" Dobs asked cautiously.

"Yes, she is in the restaurant and I am out front."

"Allison, listen to me very carefully. Nikki identified the driver that ran into her. It was Andrea's brother. And now he is dead. There's nothing to link Andrea to the accident but we know she talked to her brother, who was a real low life, right before it happened. I am concerned for your safety. Can you understand that?"

"Do the police think my Mom had something to do with it?"

"I am sitting right here with Detective Boyle. He has talked to your mother and taken a full deposition from her and there is no real evidence that she was behind it. But it sure seems like she could have been. Sure made it easier to get you, didn't it?"

"Dobs," Allison paused. "Can I please have Nikki's number? I want to talk to her."

"Sure." Dobs opened up his wallet and gave her the number. "She is undergoing a lot of therapy right now but I think she is getting better. I haven't told her you are gone yet."

"That's even better. I can tell her myself. Thanks Dobs. Give Jamie a kiss for me. Talk to you soon." Allison hung up and walked back into the restaurant. She would call Nikki later.

"So," Andrea began. "Did you talk to her?"

"I talked to Dobs. He said that your brother ran over Nikki and the police think you might have had something to do with it." Allison felt brave in such a public place.

"That's absurd. I told the detective everything he needed to know. My brother was a tweaker who probably just had too much to snort and too much to drink and ran into her that night. I had nothing to do with it. You must believe me." Andrea stared into Allison's eyes and seemed to be telling the truth.

"Okay, but I had to ask you about it. Dobs sounded so concerned when he told me about your brother." Allison felt a little better.

Andrea grabbed her hand and squeezed tightly. "I am your mother and I love you. Come on, let's go."

Once back in the van, Andrea told Allison she had a surprise for her. They drove in silence for about fifteen minutes into the streets of downtown Portland. Homeless teenagers wandered throughout the area. Many were laughing and apparently enjoying themselves. Andrea drove slowly as she spoke. "These kids all have parents at home, Allison. But they ran away to live here on the streets. Some left because they were being abused but some left just because they were mad at their parents for getting a divorce."

"Wow," said Allison. "I can't believe how many of them there are." They passed a large brightly colored graffiti covered building that had a line of kids out front.

"And that's where they line up to get their meals," Andrea continued.

"Mom, this is really sad. Can we just get back on to the highway?" Allison was hoping that her mother wasn't planning on stopping to engage some of the kids in conversation.

Andrea looked sternly at her. "I wanted you to see this. Do you understand now how lucky you are to have me back again as your mother? You will never have to be like these kids."

"Yeah, Mom. I get it. Can we just leave now?" Allison was visibly disturbed by what she had seen.

Andrea increased her speed after they made a right turn and up ahead Allison saw a sign for the interstate. In a few minutes they were on their way to Spokane and a reunion with Allison's father. Allison took out her phone and called Nikki.

It was about nine o'clock when Nikki's phone rang. She had just finished watching one of her favorite shows, *Dancing with the Stars*. A nurse had just taken her vitals and had complimented her on how well she was coming along. She reached over to her nightstand and picked up the phone.

"Nikki? It's Allison. How are you doing?" Since Dobs had not told Nikki that Allison was missing, her mood was light and she was excited to hear Allison's voice.

"I'm just fine. How are you doing? And Jamie?"

"Jamie's fine. I told Dobs that I wanted to be the one to tell you what I've done."

"What do you mean?"

"I have gone with my mother for a few days. She is taking me to meet my real father tomorrow. I'm safe and please don't be too mad at Dobs. He's been doing a great job with us and he is taking real good care of Jamie. I just need to do this now, can you understand that? I love you and appreciate everything you've done for me and I will be coming to see you soon. Are you okay?"

Nikki felt her heart racing as she tried to control what she said. "But don't you remember what happened the last time you went off with her? And I had to come get you?"

"I remember. But this time it's different. I've given it a lot of thought and I want to get to know her. Not in three years but right now. And I want to meet my dad too. Can't you understand that? It's nothing against you and Dobs. Plus you need time to recover, right? This is probably the best time for me to do it anyway, right?" Allison sounded more mature than Nikki remembered her being.

"And how long have you been gone?" Nikki began to fume internally that Dobs had not told her.

"Just since last night."

"And where are you?"

Allison paused. "On our way to see my father. I promise I'll call you back soon. I love you Nikki." She hit the end button on the small black throwaway phone.

Andrea looked over at her. "You did a great job, sweetie. Now just throw that phone out the window and I will give you another one tomorrow as soon as we get to Spokane."

Nikki stared at the telephone still in her hand as her mind raced. How dare he not call her and let her know Allison was gone! What was he thinking? But, I guess he didn't want to upset me yet. Well, fuck that. Now I'm really upset. She dialed Dobs' number but then quickly hung up. It occurred to her that maybe he wanted her to hear it from Allison instead of him. After all, she had said no to her going to spend a few days with her mom and Dobs had been somewhat open to the idea. Maybe she was being too protective about the whole thing. After all, Allison was Andrea's child, supposedly. Nikki had been nothing more than another foster parent in a long line of foster parents. True, she had adopted them last year. But apparently that didn't account for much with Allison. Why did she insist on being with that crazy bitch mother of hers if she had such a nice home with Nikki? Well, maybe it wasn't such a nice home anymore. No, that wasn't it. It was a fine home and maybe it was just that Allison wanted to get to know her real mother. "This is fucking crazy!" she said aloud as she redialed Dobs.

When he answered she was crying. "Dobs?"

"Nikki, I'm sorry but I wanted you to hear it from her."

"Well I heard it alright. Christ, she is with her right now, God knows where, and they are on their way to see her father!" Her sobbing was now subdued.

"She's almost sixteen and has her mind made up for now. Let's just try to work with her. I've been talking to Detective Boyle and he says that if Allison actually wants to be with her mother right now it will be very hard to work it as a kidnapping, even though you are her adoptive mother. I know, it sucks."

"So we just let her go?" Still sobbing.

"For now. Unless you want to get the FBI involved and Boyle advises against it until we hear more from Allison. The fact that Andrea is letting her call us shows some compassion on her part, according to him, so we should just wait until we hear back from her. But..." Dobs was careful here. "Since you are in no shape to go anywhere right now it's probably best just to wait and see what happens."

"Wait and see! Jesus Christ, Dobs. Are you serious?" Nikki knew he was but she had to let it all out.

She realized that if Allison did not want to come home and she wanted to stay with her mother for now, there was not much that could be done. "Don't you think we ought to at least alert the adoption agency about what has happened?"

"Probably so. Detective Boyle said he was obligated to notify them but it would probably look good if you called them when I get back up there on Monday morning."

"I can not believe this is happening, Dobs. Do we even know where they are? Are they even still in California?"

"Boyle says the phone call I received was from a cell phone in Portland, Oregon."

Dobs knew this would probably upset her even more.

"Portland! Well, fuck. What a mess. But at least she sounds okay, don't you think?" Nikki had stopped crying and was feeling more in control of her emotions.

"She sounded fine to me, Nikki. Listen, try to get some sleep and I will call you as soon as I hear anything. But my guess is that it won't be tomorrow. We'll call the agency when I get back up there with you, okay? I love you."

"I love you too, Dobs." Nikki hung up the phone and stared at the ceiling for a few minutes, thinking about the whole situation, before she buzzed the nurse and asked for something to help her sleep.

Dobs hung up and went in to check on Jamie, who was still sitting in front of her computer, lost in the world of social networking. The fact that Allison was gone didn't seem to have bothered her too much. "You okay, hon'?"

She looked up at him and he could see she had been crying. “Yeah, I’m okay. Is Alli okay?”

“She said to tell you she loves you and to give you a kiss goodnight.” Dobs walked over and gave her a kiss on her forehead.

“Do you think she is going to stay with her real mother, Dobs?” Jamie asked timorously.

“Don’t know. She definitely wants to get to know her some though.” He sat down on the edge of her bed. “What would you do if it was you, Jamie?”

“Stay with her of course. If she was my real mother and she loved me I would stay with her. Wouldn’t you?”

Dobs stared at Jamie without answering her as Jamie turned back to her computer monitor and her MySpace page.

CHAPTER 16

Ron Moseley stood in front of his full length mirror in the master bedroom of his house in Spokane. He was nude and admiring the reflection of his forty-four year old body in the mirror. He reached over to his dresser and grabbed his bikini cut, leopard skinned Speedos and put them on, pulling them up tightly over his long thin legs until they completely covered his genitals and very little else. He turned sideways and saw that his firm buttocks were still amply exposed. He grinned at himself in the mirror.

His lawn was not that big. Neither was the house. But it was his home and had been for over sixteen years, ever since he had broken up with Andrea. And now she was coming to visit him and she was bringing his daughter with her. He had not seen her in two years and he was really looking forward to it. She had visited him five or six times over the years, mostly when she was in Boise for an Art Festival or to do a portrait for someone.

Ron came out of the side garage door and walked over to a small shed where he kept the lawn mower. Checking for gas and finding out there was plenty, he leaned over and quickly pulled the starter cord and the engine started right up. Next, he grabbed the ear bud that was hanging from a purple ipod that protruded from the side of his Speedos and stuck it in his ear. Cranking up some Lynyrd Skynyrd, he was ready to mow, completely oblivious to any of the neighbors that often spied on him when he mowed his lawn. A few years back he had tried to do it without the Speedos but the complaints had come roaring in to the police and he was asked to stop. From then on he had kept himself covered with the Speedos.

Inside the house he was always completely nude. It was almost like a religion to him. He had discovered it years ago from a fellow science fiction writer, Ashley Flood, when she had come to visit him. She convinced him that nudity was the next fully evolved state for humans and that few really understood it yet. She lived with him for a couple of years but then finally moved back to her home in Florida. The Eastern Washington winters were too much for her. But she had made it clear he was welcome to visit at any time and he had taken her up on the offer once or twice. He also attended weekly gatherings at a small nudist colony just a few miles outside of Spokane where he was an avid swimmer and tennis player at the indoor pool and tennis courts.

But for now he was listening to *Freebird* and mowing the lawn, anxious to meet the daughter he had never seen. It bothered him a great deal that Andrea had asked him to wear clothes while they were visiting him, but he had agreed to it.

As he pushed the mower up and down the lawn, he noticed that his belly was larger than he would like for it to be. That meant he needed to cut back on some of the wine he consumed, he knew that, and it also meant he needed to be more physically active during the week when he was at home alone at his writing desk or sitting in his red leather recliner. He would write for several hours at his desk and then move to the recliner, where he kept a Styrofoam ice chest next to the chair half full of ice yet with enough room for a 1.5 liter bottle of Sangria. He would consume about one bottle each day as he read Tolkien's trilogy over and over again, memorizing entire passages that he would spew forth later in the evening when he could no longer keep his eyes on the page. And when he would occasionally have a few of his nudist friends over for a soirée, they would all admiringly stare at him as he recited the passages much to their amazement. The evening would end as several partners paired off with each other to the different bedrooms to share sexually with each other, also considered by Ron and his guests to be a more evolved state for humans.

As he finished with the lawn, it occurred to him that the next few days would demand much control from him. He would wear clothes. He would write much less and drink less wine and have no guests over. He would try to come across to his daughter as a very responsible person who also happened to be her father.

Once back inside the house he ripped off the Speedos and tossed them back on his dresser. He then began searching through dresser drawers he had not opened in years for what would be his new wardrobe for the next few days. Once he had picked out a few things, he set them down on top of the dresser and walked down the hall to what would soon be Andrea's bedroom. It was in pretty good shape but he did decide it would be a good idea to wash the sheets. After tearing them off the bed he walked down the hall to another bedroom that would be Allison's and also removed the sheets from the bed.

As he looked around Allison's room he knew this was the better room for her because the walls were covered in artwork that had been the cover art for several of his published science fiction books. It looked like a much better room for a teenager, a lot more fun and exciting. It even had a CD player and a small flat screen TV with a DVD player. He checked the player for any porn disks that might have been left in it and also cleared out the cabinet beneath the TV. She would be very happy in this room, he thought to himself as he turned and walked towards the laundry room with his arms full of dirty sheets.

While Ron was preparing the house for their arrival, Andrea and Allison were still on the road. They had been driving all night, taking turns, but they would be there soon. Allison sat in the passenger seat anxious to see a mileage sign showing how much farther it was to Spokane. Andrea stared straight ahead, as though in a trance. Allison looked out her window at the fields and trees, surprised at how barren it looked here in rural Washington. She thought back to when she was little, maybe six or seven. Before she had connected with Jamie. She was in an agency dormitory and had wondered into the kitchen area where a tall burly woman, the cook, was preparing the evening meal. She had piles and piles of potatoes on the large cutting board area next to the sink and she was ranting on and on about how much better a real Idaho potato was compared to just about any other potato. As Allison looked out the window of the van, she wondered if Idaho potatoes were really grown only in Idaho. Or were some grown here in Washington?

Then she saw the sign up ahead: SPOKANE 35 miles. "We'll be there soon, Mom."

"Yes we will sweetie."

"So my father is a writer? And he has published books?"

"Yes. Science Fiction books."

"Is he rich?"

"Not really rich. But he supports himself." Andrea wished she hadn't mentioned the nudist thing to Allison but she had wanted her to be prepared, just in case Ron didn't keep his word about wearing clothes during their visit. She could see that Allison was proud of the fact that her father was a published writer, even if it was Science Fiction.

Andrea was working on her fourth cup of coffee and her stomach was grinding from all of the caffeine. But, they were almost there. She knew it was time to take her meds but she hated taking them on an empty stomach, especially an upset empty stomach. She reached for the medicine bottle in the center console and shook a pill into her mouth, washing it down with the rest of her coffee. At least she would be able to deal with Ron rationally when they got there, even if her stomach was burning.

Allison gave her directions from a notepad after they got off at his exit and in a few minutes they were pulling into his subdivision. The homes were small ranch models, built on what looked like concrete slab foundations. But the concrete only ran around the outside of the frame of the house because in this part of the country everyone had a basement. Small, shabby shrubs grew along the front of the houses and the occasional ornamental tree looked somewhat less than ornamental. The fences were chain link and several outdoor doghouses could be seen in the backyards from the street. The neighborhood was less than what Allison had expected for a successful writer, but, she thought to herself as they pulled into the driveway, maybe the inside is nice.

Ron opened the front door wearing a black tank top t-shirt and baggy white shorts. They didn't know it at the time but he always refused to wear underwear so he had gone commando. He walked out to the car and Allison was surprised at how tall he was. "This must be my baby girl," he shouted with his arms outstretched for a hug, which she gave him with a small hesitation.

"Hi Dad." Allison looked over at Andrea and then back to him. "Is that what I should call you?"

"You can call me Dad. Or, you can call me Ron if you prefer." He was looking over towards Andrea who was just getting out of the driver's side. He began walking around the van towards her. “And here is my outlaw Mama! How you doin’ girl?”

Andrea kissed him on the cheek and said, “Grab some bags, will you. I’ve got to take a leak real bad. Come on Allison, let’s go inside. He’ll bring everything in for us.” They both smiled at Ron and turned to walk up the small flagstone path towards the front door. Allison trailed behind Andrea and studied the rundown condition of the yard and front landscaping, wondering why he didn’t take better care of the place.

Once they were all settled in at the kitchen table, Ron announced he was grilling steaks for dinner as he opened up a large 1.5 liter bottle of Sangria he had brought up from the basement. He placed three glasses on the table with a can of cold Dr. Pepper next to one of the glasses for Allison. Andrea reached out and put her hand over her glass to prevent him from pouring her any wine, saying, “It’s early, Ron. I’ll just share the soda with Alli.”

“Whatever,” Ron said as he brought out two bags of chips from the pantry and threw them on the table. “Me? I’m having some vino.”

Allison took a few sips of her soda before asking, “Dad? I mean, Ron? Can I see where I’ll be sleeping? I could really use a nap before dinner.”

“Follow me. You get the special room. Here, you’ll see.” He headed down the hall and she followed him into the room he had prepared for her. “And you got nice clean sheets I just put on.” He stared at the artwork on the walls, as did she.

“What are these pictures?” Allison asked. There were colorful drawings of planets, stars, and nebula – and several strange looking animal like creatures - all out in what appeared to be deep space. "Are these from your books?"

"They are the cover artwork from some of my books. Aren't they amazing? The publishing company sends a big poster to me each time they publish one of my books and I put 'em all up in this room." Ron stared proudly at the walls. "It's like a shrine to your father, honey."

"Thanks," Allison said as she turned down the covers. "Wake me up before dinner. I love steak!"

"You got it, kiddo. I'll bring your bag in once your Mom tells me which one it is."

"Oh, here. I'll come show you." She quickly moved back down the hall and grabbed her suitcase from where it sat on the brown tile floor of the foyer. "I got it. You go visit with Mom. I'll see you in a while." She carried the suitcase back to her room and closed the door after quickly using the bathroom right across the hall from her room. Her period had just started and she had remembered to bring some tampons in her suitcase.

After she climbed into bed she realized that Andrea had not given her a new cell phone yet. She wanted to call Jamie but couldn't. She wanted to tell her how much she missed her and how badly she wanted to see her - that she was only away on a short trip and they would both be back together again real soon.

Unable to sleep, Allison went back into the kitchen to sit at the table with Ron and Andrea, who were drinking wine and talking up old times. They were aware of her presence yet they weren't. They looked into each other's eyes as they told story after story. Ron began to tell her about his new book and it gave Allison a chance to slide away from the table and explore the rest of the house.

A door in the hallway opened up into a flight of wooden stairs leading down into the basement. Allison walked down the stairs and saw Ron's work area. His computer was on and so was a small desk lamp. "Facebook," she thought to herself as she walked over and sat down at the desk.

Once online she went to Jamie's page and sent her a quick IM. Luckily Jamie was online and answered her back immediately. "heh, sis. where are you?"

"with my mom and dad. doesn't that sound totally weird? my dad lives up here in spokane, washington and we are visiting him for a few days. r u okay? I miss u."

"i'm fine. miss u 2. dobs is leaving to go see nikki again later tonight. he says he is going to bring her back home tomorrow if he can."

"jamie? do u think they are going to send the police after me?"

"no, not dobs. I heard him talking with that detective boyle and he said they were just going to see how you did for the next few days."

"but what about when nikki comes home?"

"i don't know. r u using your dad's computer right now?"

"yeah. probably not too smart but she threw my phone away so they couldn't track us."

"yeah," said Jamie. "now they can just trace his ip address to the house you are in!"

"shit, i wasn't thinking. gotta go for now. try to keep this a secret, okay?"

"okay, sis. love you," Jamie told her before she signed out.

Allison sat in her father's desk chair and closed out Facebook, thinking to herself how stupid she had been but also sort of relieved that at least now they could find out where she was if they needed to come get her. She stood up and walked back out of the basement. She could still hear their voices from the kitchen, louder than they had been before, as she climbed the stairs. They were almost oblivious to the fact that she was not with them.

She walked in on them and asked, "Mom, are we going to be staying here awhile?"

Andrea smiled at Ron and then replied, "Well we were just talking about that."

"I was just wondering what I was going to be doing about school. Do you think they will let me transfer? When I left school Friday they didn't know I was moving. I guess Dobs called me in sick today? There's probably some paperwork or something to fill out for a transfer. Are we going to stay here in Spokane?"

"I don't know yet, sweetie." Andrea looked at Ron, who was half inebriated. "I don't think so. I wanted you to meet you father and here he is. But we will probably go back to Phoenix once I hear that Dobs and Nikki are okay with you staying with me. I have a great high school all picked out for you, and it is close to my house."

Allison looked at Ron and then back to Andrea. "Should I call Dobs or Nikki again? See what they say?"

Andrea reached into her black leather purse that hung on the back of her chair and pulled out a new black throwaway phone. "Here, sweetie. Call them. Don't say we're in Spokane but tell them you want to come live with me in Phoenix and see if they will start the paperwork."

"Okay." Allison took the phone and walked back down the hall to her room.

CHAPTER 17

Dobs made arrangements for Nikki to leave the hospital on Monday afternoon. He explained to the doctors that her daughter had been kidnapped or had run away. They told him that as long as Nikki did her exercises they had given her she should be okay to travel back home.

They were driving back to Laguna Beach on Monday evening when Allison's call came in on Dobs' cell phone. He saw who was calling and handed the phone to Nikki. Allison told her she wanted to stay at her mom's house in Phoenix but she also wanted to come home too. She was confused and frustrated with having to make a choice. "I feel so bad, Nikki. I want to see you. I want to be able to help you get better. Dobs built these really cool ramps in the front yard and I want to see you use them. And I want to be with Jamie. She's my little sister. But," she paused. "I want to get to know my mother too. This is so hard for me."

Nikki tried to sound patient and comforting even though she was furious inside. "Now Allison, of course you want to spend time with your real mother. I understand that. But I adopted you last year as my own daughter and I love you and want to make sure you do the right thing. Are you in Phoenix right now, at her house?"

Reluctantly, Allison lied. "Yeah."

"Well, Dobs got her Phoenix address from Detective Boyle. What do you say we drive on over tonight and all have breakfast together in the morning to work things out?"

Allison froze. She wanted to say yes, please come on over and we'll all talk it out. She stared around her father's half finished basement and saw pipes protruding from a wall where a bathroom had never been built. She saw piles of old of magazines stacked against another wall. She didn't know until she actually reached over and picked one up that they were mostly nudist magazines. Staring at the cover of the magazine, she said, "Well, Nikki. I don't think that's going to work with my mom's schedule tomorrow." She wanted to tell her where she was but didn't. "Maybe in a couple of days? Wouldn't it be better if you went home and saw Jamie and got used to being out of the hospital while I talk to my mom about you guys coming over to see us? Maybe you could even bring Jamie. Call her in sick for a day or two. How about that?"

Allison's suggestion made sense to Nikki. She would like to go home first and see Jamie and take a real bath in her own bathtub. They could go over on Wednesday maybe. "Okay, sweetie. You talk to her and then call me back in the morning, okay?"

Allison was relieved. "Okay, Nikki. That sounds great! I'll call you then. Love you."

"Love you too." Nikki ended the call and started to hand the phone back to Dobs.

"You know you have an unread text in here don't you?"

"From who?"

"Looks like it's from Detective Boyle. It says 911 on the subject line and the message says to call him immediately."

"When did it come in?"

"About an hour ago. We must have been passing through a no service area. Looks like there is a voicemail too."

"What does it say? My password is 9891. Put it on speaker." Dobs watched Nikki as she dialed his voicemail.

"Mr. Dobson, this is Detective Boyle. Looks like we have a lead in this thing. Apparently Andrea Perkins left her business card with a bartender when she was looking for her brother. And, the same business card just turned up at the rooming house in San Pedro where the brother was staying. It was picked up and bagged as evidence when LAPD did a sweep of his place after he was killed, but somehow it was not recorded in the log and it just turned up today when they were preparing his case file for storage. Sloppy work, I know. But, at least now we have enough to get an arrest warrant on Perkins. Which

I just got and I am contacting the authorities in Phoenix to pick her up tonight. Call me on my cell after you get this message."

Dobs and Nikki both sat silently for a moment before saying anything. Dobs spoke first. "So now what the hell are we supposed to do?"

"We have to tell Boyle that she has Allison. They need to know that before they send in the cops to pick her up." Nikki paused while thinking. "We need to get to Phoenix tonight, you realize that, don't you?"

"Of course I do. Call your Aunt Luanne and tell her we won't be home until tomorrow. But don't say anything else."

"Okay." Nikki was dialing Luanne's cell. When she got no answer she called Jamie, who did answer. "Jamie, where is Luanne?"

"She's in the bathroom, why. Are you still coming home tonight?"

"No dear, but we will be there tomorrow afternoon. And Allison will be with us too."

"Really? I just talked to her a while ago and she didn't say anything about that." Jamie sounded confused.

"You just talked to her? What did she say?"

"She just told me that she missed me and she was with her mother and her real father and things were okay."

Nikki still had the phone on speaker and when they both heard "real father" they stared at each other, a nervous apprehension sweeping over both of them at the same time. "Her real father?" Nikki asked.

"Yeah. She seemed pretty happy. We weren't really talking so I couldn't tell her how she sounded."

"What do you mean you weren't really talking?"

"We were IMing each other on Facebook. But she seemed okay. Why?"

"Well this is the first I've heard about a real father. How about you?"

"Yeah, me too. I don't think she knew anything about him. Her mom must have surprised her by taking her up there."

"Up where?" Nikki asked. "I thought they were in Phoenix. Jamie, I am worried about her. The police told us we should try to get her to come back home"

"She said she was in Spokane, Washington." Jamie's concern over Allison's safety won out over any promise she had made to Allison. "Not Phoenix." She paused before adding. "You know the police can find out exactly where she is by using her IP address, right?"

Nikki wasn't sure she understood what Jamie was saying as Dobs interjected, "That means they can trace her by the computer she was using."

"I knew that," Nikki said. "Okay, listen up Jamie. You have Aunt Luanne call me as soon as she can. And don't say anything to Allison if she contacts you again. Just tell her I really need for her to call me, okay?"

"Okay, Nikki. I will. So will I still see you tomorrow?"

"I'm not sure yet. We'll talk again later after I talk to Luanne. Love you."

"Okay, love you too," Jamie said as she ended the call.

"So, now what? We call Boyle, right?" Dobs asked.

"Yeah, we need to let him know what's going on. He can send someone to my house to do the IP trace and we can ask him what we should do. I don't know if we should go up there or just let them handle it. With her father involved – we don't know anything about him. He could be as crazy as the mother."

"You're right. We should head back home. We can be there in two hours."

Nikki called Boyle and explained everything. He agreed they should come home tonight. He could meet with them later and let them know what to do. It made good sense to Dobs and Nikki and they continued south on the 5, heading back to Laguna Beach, not saying very much to each other along the way.

CHAPTER 18

Early the next morning Allison was awakened by her father, Ron. He stood in her bedroom doorway holding three fishing poles in one hand and a tackle box in the other. "Come on girl. Time to get up. We're goin' fishing."

A tired looking Andrea stood behind him and walked into the room and sat down on the side of Allison's bed. "Wake up, sweetie. Your father's got a big day planned for us."

Allison rubbed her eyes and sat up in bed. "Where are we going?"

"Newman Lake. Let's go!" Ron was extremely excited about it and walked back down the hall towards the garage. "I already got bait out here in the garage refrigerator."

Allison looked at her mom. "Do we really have to go fishing?"

"Yes, ma'am. Its part of the deal of getting to know your dad."

"But I thought we were going back to Phoenix?"

"Maybe tomorrow, sweetie. Now, get up and I'll fix you a bowl of cereal and meet you in the kitchen. I already packed a good lunch."

On their way to the lake Ron stopped only once, and that was to get a pack of cigarettes and a six pack of beer for the cooler in the back seat that was already full of sandwiches and soda. They got to the lake in about fifteen minutes and it was beautiful, much larger than Allison or Andrea had expected it to be. There was a small boat house where you could rent a fishing boat and that's what Ron did.

They spent the first few hours out on the water fishing, catching several small mouth bass until Ron announced that they had enough fish for lunch. Then he brought the boat into a sandy beach area and everyone got out before he pulled the aluminum boat completely out of the water on to the sand, groaning as he did so.

There were small barbeque grills perched around the area and they moved to the one nearest the beached boat. Andrea set out a large blanket near the grill and began unloading things from the boat. It was about noon and the sky was clear and the temperature was pleasant, about 70 degrees. After they were all seated, Ron pulled a beer out of the cooler and rolled a soda towards Allison. "Work up quite a thirst out there, don't you girl?"

It bothered Allison that her father had grown so comfortable in calling her 'girl' instead of by her actual name but she didn't say anything about it. She watched him as he spread some newspaper on top of the blanket and began to clean the fish. Andrea walked over to the grill with a can of lighter fluid and a small bag of charcoal and very soon she had a nice fire going.

Allison watched both of them carefully, thinking that this is what her life might have been like if they had never given her away as a baby. She would have grown up with trips like this to the lake, picnics in parks and playgrounds, local carnivals, maybe even been taken to a circus or a ball game. Things she had never done. Things you did with a family. Ron worked diligently on the fish he was cleaning and Andrea scraped the old dried up food off the top of the grill. They would have done this many times before with Allison at their side. But they had chosen not to do that, not to keep her. She watched them and wondered what it must feel like to them to have her back now that so much time had passed.

She had a cold, sick feeling come over her as she watched them prepare the meal. A wave of sadness. These two people were her parents, yet they had abandoned her so they could have their own lives to themselves. How selfish of them, she thought to herself as she looked out over the water. In the distance, off to her right about a hundred yards she could see the boathouse and dock. And beyond that she could make out

Ron's car parked next to a shed. At least they weren't planning on keeping her here for some kind of campout sleepover on the beach. She looked back at Andrea and saw that she and Ron were standing by the grill cooking the fish.

Allison stretched out on the blanket and closed her eyes. She began to think about Nikki and Jamie. Dobs too. Wondering what they were doing. She drifted off into a half sleep until she heard Ron announce, "Fish are done. Let's eat."

She wasn't a big lover of fish in the first place but this grilled bass actually tasted pretty good. It would have been better with some tarter sauce and a roll but it wasn't bad by itself. "Very good," she said to both of them.

"Your daddy has always been very handy with a fishing pole, sweetie." Andrea ate frantically as though she were starving.

"So, are we all going back to Phoenix together?" Allison asked innocently.

"Well," Ron began. "I reckon you and your mother can head down there tomorrow and maybe I'll come down for a visit real soon, maybe in a week or two. How's that sound?"

"That sounds good. So Mom, are we driving straight though? How far is it?"

Andrea wiped off her mouth with a paper towel. "If we leave tonight, and take turns like we did before, we should get there tomorrow night. You can tell Nikki and Dobs. They can meet with us on Thursday for lunch."

"I'll call them tonight once we get on the road."

"That'll work. Hey, anyone up for a dip?" Andrea stood up and began taking off her clothes. At first Allison was sure she was going to strip down to nothing but then she saw the bikini she was wearing underneath.

Ron tore off his top and left his shorts on as they both raced for the water. Allison stretched out on the blanket again and closed her eyes. Saying to herself out loud, "My mom and dad."

After a couple of hours of swimming and horseplay, Andrea unpacked the cooler and passed out sandwiches. They were peanut butter on white bread with no jelly. Then she handed a beer to Ron and got out two cold cans of Coke for Allison and herself.

"How come there's no jelly on this sandwich?" Allison asked.

"Oh, they're actually a lot better for you this way, sweetie. And they're really good if you eat a banana at the same time. Here, everybody take one." She passed out the bananas.

"They're kind of dry, Mom." Allison tried not to sound like she was complaining. "But they are very good with the banana." It made her appreciate how good the fish had been earlier. She watched as Ron and Andrea ate their sandwiches and when they were looking the other way she buried half of hers in the sand.

After they were all done with the sandwiches, Ron launched the boat again and they were back to some serious fishing. Allison actually liked this part better than being on the beach because Ron made sure that everyone was quiet and that talking was kept to a minimum. "So as to not disturb the fish," he told them.

They caught a few more fish before Ron steered the boat back towards the dock. They loaded up the car and were back on the road to home by five o'clock.

When they pulled on to Ron's street about five thirty, it was still light outside. But the colored lights on top of the Sheriff's car parked in front of Ron's house were flashing red and blue. No siren, just the ominous lights. There was another police car parked with no lights on in front of it.

"What the fuck?" Ron exclaimed.

"Are you in some kind of trouble, Ron?" Andrea asked, just as they got close enough for her to see that most of the contents of her VW van had been emptied out on to his front lawn and one officer was going through everything while another female office made notes on a large clipboard.

Ron pulled into the driveway and parked his car, quickly jumping out and saying to the officers, "What are you guys doing to her stuff?"

Andrea got out of the passenger door and as soon as she did two other officers walked up to her and said, "Andrea Perkins?"

"Yes," Andrea said.

"Miss Perkins, we have a warrant for your arrest for attempted murder and conspiracy to commit murder in Orange County CA. Please put your hands behind your back."

"Allison was just getting out of the backseat of the car and the female officer who had been taking notes on the clipboard came over and asked her if she was Allison Pittilon. She had taken Nikki's last name after the adoption last year. She told the officer who she was and was gently taken by the arm and walked over to one of the police cars and placed in the backseat.

"But what about my stuff inside?" Allison asked the officer.

"Once we get her in the car you and I will go inside and get all of your stuff. You just sit tight here for a minute and I'll be right back."

"Okay." Allison sat in the backseat and watched as her mother was handcuffed and placed in the backseat of the other police car. Then the officers began questioning Ron.

After a few minutes the female officer came back and got Allison and brought her inside to get her clothes and suitcase. "So you are arresting my mother?"

"Yes, but you will be safe tonight and tomorrow you will be back where you belong. I know you don't understand everything that's going on but you are much better off and much safer coming with us tonight. Nikki Pittilon, who is your adoptive mother, paid for a plane ticket so we can send you home. You are scheduled to arrive in Orange County tomorrow at about noon.

When they left the house with Allison carrying her suitcase, the one police car that carried Andrea was gone. The other officer was still talking to Ron while he was unloading the fishing poles and cooler from his car. Allison asked, "That man is my father. Can I go say goodbye to him?"

The female officer walked over towards Ron with Allison and let her say goodbye before they walked out towards the car in the street. Allison turned back and said, "Thanks for the fishing trip, Dad."

"You're welcome, girl. You're welcome," he answered and then he continued unloading his car. After a pause he looked back up and screamed back to her. "Allison, maybe ask your folks if they mind me coming to see you once in a while?"

Allison turned back and smiled at Ron. "I will. Goodbye, Dad."

The ride back to the police station in downtown Spokane was quiet at first. Allison watched the female officer driving the car and wondered if she had any kids of her own. Finally she said something to her, "So, I get to go home tomorrow?"

"That's right. Your mother bought a ticket for you. She said she would have come herself but you would understand why she didn't."

"Yeah. She's in a wheelchair," Allison explained.

"I know she is. But the good news is she said she may be getting better from her treatments." The officer stared straight ahead as she talked.

"So you spoke to her today?"

"We had to know what to do with you, didn't we? So we didn't have to hold you over here in Spokane. I told her we had a nice facility you could stay in but she explained to me that you've already spent enough time in facilities and it was best we just get you back home to her."

"What is your name?" Allison asked.

"I am Officer Brenda Miller. But you can call me Brenda."

"Thank you, Brenda." Allison looked out the passenger window as she asked, "And what's going to happen to my real mom?"

"She is being charged and sent back to Orange County."

"On the same plane as me?"

"Goodness gracious no. She'll be with us a few days and then we'll be sending her back down there to the authorities. Looks like she went a little too far trying to get you back. They think she had something to do with your new mom getting hurt." Officer Miller knew she probably shouldn't be saying anything about it to Allison but she didn't hesitate.

"Probably so. She really wanted me to be with her, I know that. We were going to live in Phoenix. She had a real good school picked out for me too. But, I think there's something wrong with her. She takes these pills all the time for bipolar." Allison felt very bad about Nikki's injury but she still had feelings for her real mother.

"Well, it's all going to work out just fine." Officer Miller slowed down as she entered the parking garage, saying, "And here we are, safe and sound."

"So I sleep at the police station tonight? In a cell?"

"No, dear. Some folks from Child Services are going to put you up for the night and I will pick you up in the morning. They have a nice room all ready for you at their agency home. It's not too far from the station here."

"Can't I just stay up all night in a waiting room here at the station? I really don't want to go to an agency home. Or could I just spend the night with you?" Allison's voice had grown apprehensive.

"Let me talk to them when we get inside and I will do what I can for you." Officer Miller smiled warmly at Allison, which made her feel a little better. They got out of the car and walked across the parking lot to the station entrance.

"What about my stuff?" Allison asked.

"We'll just leave it in the car for now, okay?"

"Okay by me." Allison was relieved.

Once inside, Allison was taken into a nice office with two empty desks, a few chairs placed in front of them, and lots of plants on the window sill that looked out over the street. Through a large window on the other side of the room, she could see across the main floor of the station. Officer Miller told her to sit tight and she would be back shortly.

She was still sitting there patiently fifteen minutes later when she saw the doors at the main entrance open up and Andrea being led in by two detectives, her hands in cuffs and her face strained and panic-ridden. Allison stood up and walked over to the window to get a better view. As she was standing there staring towards her mom, Officer Miller returned. "Good news, Allison. You get to sleepover at my house tonight. It's against the rules but the chief said it was okay."

Turning towards Brenda, Allison said as she smiled, "Thanks Brenda. Guess it's a good thing we left all my stuff in your car."

After a good night's sleep at Brenda's condo in the guest bedroom, Allison was awakened at eight-thirty by Brenda at her door saying, "Get up and get a shower and we'll have time to stop for donuts on the way to the airport."

At the airport, while waiting in line at the Southwest gate, she spoke to Brenda for the last time as she thanked her for the donuts and everything else she had done for her. Then it was her turn to board the plane.

The flight was smooth and Allison had a lot of time to think about what had happened to her, and how grateful she was for having Dobs and Nikki to take care of her. And how much she missed Jamie. As the plane entered the airspace over Newport Beach as it prepared to land at John Wayne Airport, the pilot made the usual joke about how they would be swinging out over the Pacific just briefly to avoid any noise pollution for the wealthy folks directly below them.

Nikki and Dobs were waiting for her at the gate with Jamie by their side. Nikki was operating a very high-tech wheelchair and held her arms out towards Allison for a hug. Dobs put his hands on Allison's shoulders while she was hugging Nikki and then felt her start to rise up to also give him a hug. Jamie was hugging Allison from behind as she embraced Dobs. Quite a homecoming, Allison was thinking to herself.

On the drive back to Laguna Beach, Allison answered their questions as best as she could, told them a little about the father she had met, and kept thanking them for being there for her. Once back at the house and resting quietly in her own bedroom, Allison began to cry, eventually crying herself to sleep.

CHAPTER 19

Andrea's trial was scheduled for mid-November and it was now early October. Allison had adjusted to being back home nicely and had even made a new best friend at school named Ruby and possibly a boyfriend named Josh. Tenth grade was easy for her. The few days she had missed while she was with Andrea didn't affect her grades at all. Nikki had told the school she was out with the flu and was able to get all of her make up work for her. Jamie was struggling along with her last year in middle school but was looking forward to attending high school the following year with Allison. Dobs was enjoying his early retirement and helping with Nikki's therapy and recuperation. None of them thought too much about the trial that was rapidly approaching.

Andrea thought mostly of the trial from her small cell she shared with another prisoner in the Orange County Jail. Her public defender, Brian Cantrell, visited her every week and tried to come up with some kind of defense. He kept telling her that all they had against her was circumstantial evidence. But still, Andrea thought of nothing else. She knew she was guilty but she couldn't see how they would ever prove it. Just because her brother had been in possession of her business card.

The medicine they were giving her was not the right kind either. The prison doctor had insisted on a different prescription that was cheaper since it was available as a generic. It didn't work the same. It kept her from feeling too depressed but it sapped her of all energy.

She spent her days in a small six by nine foot cell that had one small window overlooking the side parking lot and The Block at Orange beyond that, an upscale outdoor mall that she had been to many times over the years. She had stood in the mall parking lot and looked out across The City Drive and seen the Orange County Jail looming in the distance. Now the picture was reversed. She had to stand up on a folded bed mattress to see anything outside the window but this kept her occupied for much of the day.

She would try to make out the cars with teenage girls in them as they parked and walked towards the mall entrance. One day she might see Allison coming to the mall with some friends. She knew she would never be able to make out any faces, but at least she could imagine she was seeing her. And would Allison stop in the parking lot and gaze out across The City Drive and realize her mother was locked up here in this tiny little room?

When she was not standing up to look outside she was lying down on her bunk. She had taken the top bunk so she could stare at the little patch of blue sky that came through the small window all day long. And the darkness that filled it at night. Her cellmate, Madge, a black girl in her early twenties, kept to herself. Somehow she had smuggled in an ipod and she spent most of her time on the bunk below just listening to her music.

After sharing the cell with Madge for about a week, Andrea had short circuited one night when they missed her medicine. She had screamed at Madge and terrified her with facial grimaces and vacant eyes. The next day Madge was moved out of her cell and they didn't replace her. Andrea now had the six by nine foot cell all to herself.

One hour a day they were allowed to go outside to the courtyard to get some exercise. Even though she didn't feel like going outside, Andrea would still force herself to follow her cell neighbors in a straight line as they walked outside at two o'clock to get fresh air and exercise. But mostly Andrea would just sit on a bench until the hour had passed, contemplating her freedom she was sure she would win in court.

One Monday morning in late October, while Andrea was staring out her little window, Dobs received a phone call form Detective Boyle. He wanted to have a meeting later that day to discuss the trial. Dobs agreed that he would have Nikki and Allison with him when he showed up later that day in Boyle's office.

Detective Boyle sat at his desk and looked across at Nikki in her wheelchair, looking hopeful, with Dobs and Allison sitting next to her. "So, we need to discuss what's going to happen here. And, by the way, Nikki, I hope you are feeling much better?"

"Much better. I can actually move my toes and feel my knees." Nikki looked at Dobs, silently thanking him. "So what is it we need to prepare for Detective Boyle?"

"Well, you know we have some pretty solid evidence that she talked with her brother prior to him running you down. But we don't really have any hard evidence that she paid him or asked him to do it. So, she could walk. I just want you all to be aware of that." Boyle looked down to a file on his desk. "And then, of course, there is the mental health issue."

"What do you mean?" Nikki asked.

"Well," Boyle began. "It seems that Andrea Perkins has been being treated by a psychiatrist for the last fifteen years for bipolar disorder. I spoke with her attorney to discuss a possible plea bargain and he brought up this bipolar issue. Apparently, legally at least, even if she had spoken to her brother about getting rid of you, or even paid him to do so, her mental condition at the time could put the whole thing into question."

Dobs spoke before anyone else had a chance. "You mean to say that she may be released after all this? What about the kidnapping of Allison here. She came right in through the bedroom window and took her."

"But you did not report it as a kidnapping so it looks like she just snuck out of the house to go see her mom. Not good enough."

CHAPTER 19

Dobs continued, "Look, the woman is crazy, sorry Allison, and if they let her out she will just come back and try to take her again. What can we do?"

"A confession would help. If she would just admit what she had done. But I don't think that's in the cards. So, we either need better evidence, or a plan to deal with what you are going to do if they let her out."

"What do you mean, a plan?" Nikki asked.

"I mean, you guys may want to consider moving away for a few years. To get away from her to a place where she can not find you, at least until Allison is older."

Dobs looked pissed. "Like where, Costa Rica?"

"No," Boyle continued. "Just someplace far away from here with no forwarding address. If I can't get probation for her I can certainly request a restraining order. But, based on past history, I don't think that will stop her. You may need to just pack up everything and leave the state."

"And what if we can just get some evidence. Is there anything from the private investigator we hired that you can use?"

"Sorry, not really. It basically comes down to whether or not the prosecutor can break her on the stand and get her to confess to what she did." Boyle sat back in his chair, feeling like he had covered everything he needed to cover.

Dobs and Nikki looked at each other in silence. Allison had a question for the detective. "So do you think they will let her go?"

"They may feel like she did nothing wrong. Unless she actually confesses."

"Will she come back and try to get me to go with her again?" Allison sounded fearful as she spoke.

"She might. That's why I'm suggesting you all might have to find a new place to live and hope she stays away."

"Or, I could just go with her and they could stay where they are, right?" Allison looked at Dobs and Nikki as she asked this.

Detective Boyle hesitated before answering. "Well, I suppose if she were found to be not guilty, and your adoptive mother here agreed to give you back, the court might approve of her taking custody of you. But only if Nikki here agreed to it, which I can't believe she would agree to. Nikki?" Boyle looked at Nikki.

"Of course I wouldn't agree to it. If we have to, we can all move away. The woman is mentally unstable and I love you, Alli. Can't you see that?"

"I know you do. But I hate to have you leave everything you have here and start all over someplace else just because of me." A tear ran down Allison's face as she spoke.

"Well," Dobs stood up. "We're not going anywhere for now. So let's just wait and see how the prosecutor handles this in court. Detective Boyle, thank you for your time and all of your help." He stood behind Nikki's wheelchair as he finished speaking and said, "Let's go guys."

Once outside and into the car, they didn't say anything for a while. Then Dobs spoke first, saying "Olive Garden anybody?"

CHAPTER 20

Andrea's attorney, Brian Cantrell, was waiting for a call back from the District Attorney's office. He sat at his desk and nervously fidgeted with a pencil, taking a break to doodle on his notepad before he began to fidget again. He was hoping to work out a plea bargain before the trial was set to begin the next morning. There had been a couple of times when he thought it was all settled and that Andrea would plead guilty to a minor conspiracy charge and be freed on probation, but each time it had fallen apart at the last minute. This was the final call. It would either be probation or a trial. Andrea had refused to accept any amount of jail time. She had reluctantly agreed to probation if it meant she would be released. When the phone call came in and the offer was for two years probation and weekly psychiatric counseling for a year, Cantrell knew she would go for it.

Andrea sat in her cell and stared out at the little patch of blue sky. On the walls around the small window she had drawn intricate artwork that complimented her view, long green tassels of branches falling down from plants that carried small purple and pink flowers. They had let her use colored chalk for her drawing because it could be easily removed and the staff psychiatrist had felt the therapy was good for her.

She was startled when she heard her door opening and Brian Cantrell entered the cell, staring at her artwork. "Very beautiful, Andrea." Then, he looked at her and said, "We need to talk."

He slowly explained the terms of the plea bargain to her and was stunned when she accepted it immediately, as long as it was acceptable for her to go back to Phoenix and complete her probation there. "They still can't prove a thing but I need to get out of here," she said. "Take the offer. When can I leave?"

"Once the judge signs off on accepting a felony conspiracy charge tomorrow morning you should be able to leave. And they did agree to let you go back to Phoenix. Fortunately for you, California and Arizona have an Interstate Compact on probation as long as it is for a class 3 felony or less. So you can go home tomorrow." Brian looked at Andrea and saw a distant and troubled look in her eyes as he said goodbye.

After he left her cell, her mind began to race with possibilities. She would go back to Phoenix and bury herself in her artwork. She would forget about trying to get Allison back, at least for now. Or maybe after a short time had passed, she could ask Nikki if Allison could just come visit her for a few days. Or, better yet, maybe she could sell her new house in Arizona and move back to Orange County. Maybe Nikki would let Allison stay with her every other weekend. And her mind continued to go over all of the possibilities as she waited for night to fall over her small window in the wall.

The following morning she received another visit from her attorney. She was being released. Her van had been transported from Spokane to Orange County by Ron, who had contacted Brenda Miller with the Spokane Police Department and found out where to have it shipped. It had been sitting in the parking garage below the building since shortly after Andrea's arrival. Cantrell told her how lucky she was that they had let her keep it parked in the garage. Ron had paid $300 for a three month parking pass but she didn't know that. She was just happy it was there.

Once fully checked out and released, she carried her purse and small bag with her down to the lower level of the parking garage where she was told her van was parked. She climbed in and tried to start it with the key they had given her but the engine wouldn't turn over. She climbed out of the driver's seat and stood in the middle of the cold concrete lot until she finally saw someone walking out of the building exit doors. It was a young man in his mid-twenties, who had just gotten off work and he responded eagerly when Andrea asked him if he had any jumper cables. Five minutes later she was driving out of the garage into the warm, afternoon sun. It was

November but the sky was blue and the temperature was in the 70s.

Andrea turned on City Drive and checked her gas. The tank was full. She saw the entrance ramp for the 22 and took the 22E ramp towards Riverside. She would follow the 5 up to the 10 and be in Phoenix before ten o clock that night.

Once on the interstate she realized how hungry she was and stopped at a Jack in the Box for a burger and curly fries in Palm Springs. After eating she reached into her purse and got another pill. She was going to do it right this time. No more on and off with the meds. She would just focus on her new house and her artwork. She could work on seeing Allison later. She began to realize how lucky she was that she had been released. If they had come up with any evidence linking her to her brother's assault on Nikki she would be in a women's prison for the next twenty or more years. But, now she was free. She felt a euphoria begin to build in her and she couldn't wait to get home. The cell phone in her purse had died a long time ago or she would have called Ron to thank him for sending the van. She would call him when she got home. For now she just kept her eyes on the empty interstate in front of her and her thoughts on how wonderful her life would be back in Phoenix.

When she arrived at nine thirty, she was struck with how dark the house was, not a light on anywhere. This was odd because she had set up an automatic bill pay for her mortgage and her utilities before leaving. And she had put the lights on a timer. She had almost asked a neighbor to watch the house but had been in such a hurry to go get Allison she had neglected to do that. She pulled into the driveway and pressed the garage door opener on the visor and the door opened and a light went on in the garage. Maybe the timer had short circuited on the other lights. At least her power was on.

Once inside, she took a shower that lasted until all of the hot water was gone. Then she went to the kitchen and put some water on to boil for some pasta. Tomorrow she would do the grocery shopping. Tonight, pasta and a jar of Ragu would be all she needed.

She walked down the hall carrying her bowl and stopped briefly outside of the room she had prepared for Allison. A soft rose colored bulb burned in the lamp on her nightstand. The room was lovely with the painting and decorating Andrea had done but it struck her now as painfully sad that her daughter wasn't here to enjoy it. She walked over and turned off the lamp and closed the bedroom door as she walked out, heading down the hall to her own room.

She sat up in her bed eating her bowl of spaghetti and watched the ten o'clock news. Then she watched a little of David Letterman before she turned off the lights and went to sleep, a peaceful sleep she had not had in months.

The next morning Andrea was awake by eight and on her way to the grocery store. She returned an hour later with plenty of groceries and fresh dairy and as she put everything away it struck her that she really needed to check her email. It had been months! She probably had job offers just waiting for her to respond to. After making herself a fresh cup of coffee, she walked to her study, turned on her computer, and began to sort through everything. Three weddings had come and gone since she left and the next one was coming up in late November, in Denver, Colorado. She responded to the email and told them she would need round-trip plane fare and a nice room for the night plus $1,500 for the portrait, which she would complete in just a few hours following the wedding. This job offer was a referral from a previous customer she had done a portrait for in Charlotte, North Carolina.

She continued reading her emails and eventually came to one from Allison. It was one she had sent back in August before Andrea had gone to get her.

Hi Mom,

I really appreciate you getting in touch with me, and I really would like to get to know you better. But I think I ought to stay here for a few more years until I finish school. Then, maybe I could come and see you. I hope you like your new home in Phoenix.

Love
Allison

CHAPTER 21

Dobs and Nikki spent countless hours on the internet trying to find the ideal place for them to move, having decided that it would be a lot easier on everyone, especially on Nikki, if they didn't have to worry about Andrea showing up at their door. Allison had agreed to not contact her mother until she graduated from high school. They would move to a new city in a new state and start their lives all over again.

Since Dobbs had basically retired, his only concern was being someplace convenient enough for his daughter Dawn and his new son-in-law, Tim, to come visit him. After much discussion and research, it was decided that their new home would be in Denver, Colorado. Particularly Douglas County on the southeast side of town, where the school scores were the highest and the homes looked the most like California. The same builder who had developed most of Mission Viejo in Orange County had also developed an area south of Denver called Highlands Ranch. It actually looked like Mission Viejo, except for the majestic Rockies and foothills along the horizon and the clear (and clean) blue skies.

Nikki leased her house in Laguna Beach to Paul for a very reasonable rent, with the understanding that if Andrea ever showed up he would simply chase her away without telling her anything about where they had moved. He moved in two days before the scheduled trial and Dobbs, Nikki, Jamie, and Alli were on their way to Colorado in a new Acura SUV Dobbs had just purchased that was wheelchair friendly and had all the special driving controls that Nikki would need should she decide she wanted to drive. It was a beautiful dark burgundy color with tinted windows. The day they set out for Colorado, Nikki had packed lots of drinks and snacks in a cooler in the back. They had waited until the United Van Lines moving van pulled away from her house before they actually got on the road. They knew they would be there before their furniture but Dobs had already booked a few nights at the Marriott in Lone Tree, right next to Highlands Ranch. They would have a mini vacation before they moved in to the rental house Dobs had already leased from a CraigsList ad.

The house was located about a half a mile from Highlands Ranch High School and the middle school was right next to it. The photos and virtual tour they had seen of the house had impressed everyone. It was about

3000 square feet and had a finished basement and a hot tub on the deck. And, the bathrooms were already handicap equipped with large metal support bars mounted on the side walls of the tub and shower. There was even a small ramp leading up from the garage into the kitchen door. They had all agreed it was meant to be when Dobs initially showed them the listing photos.

They all stayed in the Marriott while they were waiting on the moving van to get there. Dobbs took Allison and Jamie to their respective schools and met with the guidance counselor to get them registered to start classes the following week. They took the light rail into downtown Denver and Nikki was very happy with the accommodations that were available for the handicapped in the different restaurants and shops they visited along the Sixteenth Street Mall.

After waiting a few days for the movers and having some fun while waiting, Dobs got the phone call that the movers would be at their new house at nine o'clock on Friday morning. That was perfect, Nikki thought to herself. They would have all weekend to unpack and the girls could start school on Monday and hopefully make some new friends. Fortunately neither one of them had developed any close friendships in the short time they had lived with Nikki in Laguna Beach, so it hadn't been that difficult for them to move away. They were both already talking about how beautiful Colorado was and how excited they were about starting school.

By Saturday morning most of the house was filled with their furniture from California and almost half the boxes were unpacked, thank to Dobs and Allison mostly. They had stayed up until 2 AM unpacking boxes and breaking them down. It was now time for some R&R according to Dobs as he walked out to the deck into the surprisingly warm November morning and turned on the hot tub. As it bubbled and spurted what looked like very clean water into the tub, the girls both ran to their rooms to put on their suits and Dobs turned to Nikki who was sitting in her wheelchair with a cup of coffee in her hand watching the tub fill. "Wow!" Dobs exclaimed.

"Wow is right, Dobs. We made it. Thanks to you. The girls are happy and it's beautiful here. Look over there." She was pointing to the Rocky Mountains along the distant horizon. "Wow is right."

"And Monday, after we get the girls to school, we head down the main road about five miles to the Steadman-Hawkins Clinic for your check up. You know, that's where all the famous skiers go, and all the Bronco sports injuries are treated there."

"I know. I read the brochure, remember?" Nikki smiled at him, rubbing her legs. "You know I do seem to be getting some feeling back down there."

Dobs walked over and knelt down next to her and picked her up. "What are you doing?"

"I'm carrying you inside to get your suit on. We're all going into this thing once it gets full. The waters already hot and it's gotta be good for you, right?"

"Right." Nikki smiled at him and kissed him on the lips while he held her in his arms, just as the girls came running back out to the deck.

"Don't get in until I get back!" Dobs told them.

CHAPTER 21

"Can't we just dangle our feet in the water?" Jamie asked excitedly.

"I guess so. I'll be back in a flash." He said as he carried Nikki into the house.

The rest of the weekend was full of smiles and laughter, and as Dobs watched all three of his girls he knew they had done the right thing by coming here. There was even a Schwab office in Greenwood Village if he decided to go back to work. But for now he was at peace. The blood pressure spikes he was having in California seemed to have disappeared since his stress level had gone down so much.

The thought of them still living in Nikki's house in Laguna with the daily risk of a surprise visit from Andrea totally freaked him out. Thank God they had moved away. Now, starting on Monday, he could concentrate on getting Nikki's therapy back in full swing.

On Sunday night as they sat out on the deck watching the sunset, Nikki asked him to bring her guitar to her. She hadn't played in a long time but she wanted to sing a particular song that had been running through her head all day. *Diamonds and Rust* by Joan Baez.

"You know," she began as she tuned her guitar. "Baez wrote this song about Bob Dylan a long, long time ago. The words reflect how I sometimes feel about you, Dobs. I get afraid that you will leave me, move on to someone else. I know you won't do that but the fear is still there." She began playing the song.

When she finished this song she played a few Joni Mitchell songs from the period in the 70s when she had first met Dobs. As Dobs listened carefully to the words and watched her play, he felt his eyes begin to moisten as he realized how much she really loved him.

Later that evening, after the girls were asleep, Nikki and Dobs made love for the first time since she had been injured. She held him tightly as he entered her and clung to him as they both reached a climax at the same time, smiling intensely that she was actually able to feel him inside of her again.

The next morning, on their way to the clinic, they dropped the girls off at school. Jamie, first, at the middle school. Then Allison at the high school. Jamie was actually less anxious about her new school than was Allison. She jumped out of the car and waved goodbye as she walked through the main entrance doors of the school, her new schedule and map in hand.

Allison, on the other hand, was very nervous about starting her new school. Once she was dropped off she waited until most of the other kids had entered the building before she slowly wandered in the main door. The security guard at the front desk greeted her, remembering her from the other day when she had met with the guidance counselor. She smiled and said hello to him as she thought about how strange it was having a security guard at such a nice high school in such a nice neighborhood. But, she had read about the Columbine shootings and knew that the schools here in Denver were extra careful about things after that had occurred. The guidance counselor had mentioned it the day they registered, telling them that Columbine High School was only about ten miles away - and also in a very nice neighborhood.

CHAPTER 21

Once classes began, Allison became more comfortable with everything. She had been assigned a mentor, Holly, to help her find her way around the campus for the first few days. Holly was a junior and two years older than Allison. When lunch time came around, Holly joined her in the cafeteria and tried to make her feel comfortable.

So far, none of the kids in her classes had been especially friendly or unfriendly towards Allison. They were all actually pretty nice to her and this surprised her a little. One girl she met named Jordan had asked her if she wanted to hang out after school at her house. Allison told her she would check with her mom and let her know. But after lunch, when she saw Jordan again, she told her that her mother wanted her to go straight home today - even though she had never called Nikki about going over there. It was too soon to be hanging out with someone she barely knew.

Later that day, when classes were just about over, she decided she would get serious about her education. She would pay attention in all of her classes, take good notes, and try to get a high GPA so she could get into a good college. She knew she would eventually make some friends but for now she would just concentrate on her academics.

When she got home from school, Nikki asked her how her first day had gone and she told her it had gone great, that she had already made a new friend named Jordan and she really liked her new school mentor, Holly. Then she went into her room and began to work on some homework. After about a half an hour had passed, she began to wish she had gone over to Jordan's house. Maybe tomorrow.

Jamie came bursting into her room. "I love my new school! Do you like yours?" She was wearing a bathing suit, apparently ready for the hot tub again.

"I don't think Dobs will let you go in by yourself." Allison said to her before answering her question. "Yeah, I like my new school too. Did you make any new friends?"

"Tons. I even got invited to a party this weekend."

"I doubt they will let you go, unless they talk to the parents first."

"Well, duh. Of course they will talk to the parents. Want me to see if you can come too?" Jamie wanted Allison to be as happy as she was.

"No, I might be doing something with my new friend Jordan. She's pretty cool. Maybe a movie night and a sleepover. Not sure yet."

"Well, if you change your mind, let me know. Want to get your suit on?" This way Jamie was sure they would let her go into the hot tub without an adult around.

Allison hesitated and looked at her textbook for a few seconds. "Oh, why not? Let's do it!"

Nikki watched the girls soak in the hot tub from the kitchen window. Her day at the Steadman Hawkins Clinic had been terrific. She even told the doctors about her restored feeling down below and they had assured her that this was a very positive sign.

Her therapist had taught her a few new exercises and Dobs had enjoyed reading a book from his new Kindle in the waiting area while she was being treated. Afterwards, they ate a wonderful lunch of French Onion Soup and Caesar Salad at Mimi's café.

Nikki had also made a friend today. Cindy, in her mid twenties, was about to get married at Roxborough Country Club the following week. She told Nikki about the giant red rock formations that loomed over the golf course and all of the wild deer that roamed freely around the outside of the clubhouse. She had told Nikki to have Dobs drive her over to see it. It was very close to Highlands Ranch. And if she felt like it, they were both invited to the wedding and reception, even though it was such a short notice.

Cindy also used a motorized wheelchair and had a similar injury to Nikki's. She had received it in an auto accident with her fiancé, who had been spared any physical injury. He had been driving and he blamed himself for it all even though another car had run a red light and hit them.

Nikki excitedly told Dobs all about it and he agreed that it might be nice if they went, they might make some new friends. They would also drive out to Roxborough this weekend and check it out since it sounded so spectacular. And the wedding reception sounded like it might be a lot of fun as long as the weather was good, so they would definitely RSVP for that.

Cindy had told Nikki all about the details of the wedding she and her mother had planned. The bridesmaid dresses, her cute little nephew who would be the ring bearer, her husband's best friend from Atlanta would be the best man, the really cool DJ she had found. She had told her nearly everything about the wedding, everything except the part about the portrait artist her father-in-law had hired, who was flying in from Arizona to do a wonderful wedding portrait of the bride and groom.

CHAPTER 22

Andrea was preparing for her next out of town wedding trip. She had been in her house in Phoenix for about two weeks and had been seeing her probation officer and psychiatrist each week. She was taking the medication that she was being given. As she packed her suitcase, she decided to go take a quick look at the weather channel, just to see if there were any early winter storms that might interfere with her trip to Denver.

Of course, she had to get permission from her probation officer each time she had to leave the state for business. It had taken several days for him to get this trip approved, making her wonder why going to Denver for a one day job was such a big deal.

She knew that Allison and her family had left California. She had asked Ron to try to contact Allison and he had been told by some guy on the phone that they had all left town and didn't leave a forwarding address, that he was just a renter and paid the rent to a property management company in Newport Beach. Paul had thought that by embellishing the story a little it would make it more believable, when in fact, it simply made Ron more interested in getting the name of the property management company. Frustrated, Paul had told him it was none of his damn business and hung up on him.

When Ron told Andrea what he had learned from Paul, she asked him to call him back and ask again. He could say he had to forward some paperwork to Dobs. Ron tried to call back but Paul had changed the number and all he got was a disconnected message. When he reported this back to Andrea, she thanked him "for nothing" and hung up.

Andrea stopped at the hall mirror to look at herself. She had never really liked the way she looked when she got angry. She tried to smile at herself. No good. She was pissed. She wanted to know where Allison was, even if it meant upsetting her parole officer, who had told her that under no circumstances was she to try and contact her. She stuck out her tongue at herself and gave herself the finger before she walked back towards the bedroom and began packing her suitcase.

She had passed Allison's bedroom on the way down the hall and just ever so quickly looked inside. Everything was perfect, just as she had left it. What teenage girl would not want such a cool bedroom?

CHAPTER 22

As she packed her suitcase, she thought about the short time she had been able to spend with Allison and how special it had been for her. The trip up to Spokane had been so important for the mother-daughter bonding she had desperately sought. And having Allison meet her real father had added even more to the moment. Allison now knew that she truly did have a real family. A real mom and a real dad.

Andrea thought about how Christmas was only a month away and how wonderful it would be if they could all be together and have a beautiful Christmas tree right out there in the living room, with decorations hanging throughout the house. Of course, it would not be a white Christmas since they were in Phoenix, but it would be so beautiful anyway. She would have Ron put up some reindeer and a sleigh that actually lit up with colored lights for the front yard. She could even paint a family Christmas portrait!

She tried calling Ron on her way to the airport but could not reach him. "God knows what he's up to!" she said to herself in the backseat of the cab. She decided she would call him from Denver.

Her flight from Phoenix was a smooth one and she landed at Denver International Airport and rented a car at the National Car Rental kiosk. She chose a Taurus, big enough to keep all of her painting supplies in and it had a built in navigational system, which she would need. Driving out of the parking garage she was struck with the beauty of the snow capped Rockies along the western horizon as she followed the directions from her navigator. She was at Staybridge Suites in Highlands Ranch, where she had booked a room in advance, in about forty minutes.

The wedding was the following day so she had some time on her hands to explore the area. She found a large mall about a mile away and decided to eat at the Cheesecake Factory and then maybe do some window shopping. It was an elegant mall called Park Meadows and she thought she might even find an art gallery or two on the upper level.

After dinner she rode the escalator up and began to wander around. That's when she thought she caught a glimpse of Allison and another girl walking along through the mall only about fifty feet away.

Andrea froze and stared at the girls as they stepped on to the down escalator. As they began moving down, Andrea rushed over to the top of the escalator and tried to get a better look, but their backs were turned to her and she couldn't be sure. She got on the escalator and followed the two girls into a Borders bookstore. They moved quickly through the store and out the other side where they were picked up by a large burgundy colored SUV that was waiting for them there. It couldn't have been her, she thought to herself. She turned around and walked back through the store towards the escalator and back to the upper level of the mall.

Trying to enjoy all of the wonderful shops that were up there was difficult with her mind now focused on Allison. She did find a small gallery and spent a few minutes there talking to the owner about her artwork and why she was in town, even giving him her business card with her website address so he could look at some of her work. After leaving the store she was ready to head back to her hotel and get a good night's rest before the wedding.

The morning air the next day was crisp and the sky was a bright blue, perfect for an outdoor reception at the Roxborough country club. Andrea drove through the entrance and was immediately struck by the bright orange and red colors of the large rock formations that stood hundreds of feet high, towering over the golf course. It reminded her of The Painted Desert. There was a bustle of activity going on as she parked her car near the rear of the building and began unloading her materials. She used a 3X5 foot mural for most of her wedding portraits, which she had fed-exd to the club a few days in advance. The rest of her art supplies were in two carrying cases she had brought with her. As she got everything out of the car and began walking through the back entrance, she was greeted by a security guard. He checked her name off on a list and told her where she could set up.

She would begin the painting after the bride and groom arrived from the church. First she would have them seated for a series of photographs and then they would be free to mingle at the reception. If she needed them again for any detail work she would simply send for them. It was about ten thirty when she found the room next to the kitchen which was to be her work area. She saw the wrapped mural leaning against the wall as she began to unfold her easel from one of her bags. She was excited and ready to go to work.

At eleven o'clock the guests began to arrive and Andrea saw the bride and groom for the first time. She had never done a wedding portrait before with the bride in a wheelchair and it occurred to her that she could offer to do the painting with or without the chair in the picture. She would let them choose.

Cindy looked radiant as she wheeled herself through the crowd, with her groom at her side, towards Andrea's work area. After a few words were exchanged, it was decided that the picture would be done with both of them seated and no sign of the chair in the portrait.

Cindy and her husband moved back out to the main floor just as Dobs, Nikki, Jamie, and Allison were arriving. The two girls were more interested in watching the band set up outside so Dobs let them do that while he and Nikki were greeted by the bride and groom and were told to look for a table with their name on it.

Outside, Allison and Jamie watched as the band unpacked their instruments and set up on the stage that overlooked the garden area next to the first tee of the golf course. The girls had never been to a wedding before and it had been beautiful. Now, they were more than ready for the reception party.

Inside, Andrea was receiving a call from Ron on her cell phone. "Where have you been? I called you three times."

"I wanted to have the correct information for you," Ron explained. "I think I found out where they moved to."

"And how did you do that?" Andrea was skeptical.

"Through a fellow writer friend of mine in Newport Beach whose wife works for the Unified School District in Orange County. They transferred the girl's records to a school district in Douglas County, Colorado. City is Highlands Ranch." Ron sounded very proud of himself. "Not bad?" he added, fishing for a compliment.

"Yeah, if only you knew." Allison stared at the empty mural on her easel, realizing that the girl at the mall last night was probably Allison. "You did very well, Ron. Now, let me blow your mind. Guess where I am for this assignment?"

"What do you mean?"

"I am in Douglas County at a wedding reception right now, as we speak. Shit, I've got to calm down." Andrea reached in her purse for a Xanax. "Ron, are you still in Spokane?"

"Yeah, why?"

"Oh, I'm just wondering what I might do if I run into her."

"Well, don't you dare bring her up here again. I get enough grief from the heat as it is."

"That's just because you don't wear clothes enough would be my guess. But, don't worry. I won't bring her back there. I won't bring her anywhere. I just want to see her and say hello. Can you get me an address?"

"No can do. They were staying in a local hotel when the transfer paperwork went through. Don't know where they are. But Allison's school is Highlands Ranch High School. I'm sure you could start there. Anyway, good luck and be careful." Ron hung up.

Allison was still staring at the blank canvas of the mural when she heard Cindy ask her how things were going and if she needed anything. She turned around and looked into her eyes and saw how happy she was, even in the motorized wheelchair. Andrea thought to herself, "How can this woman be so happy and so at peace with everything?" Fortunately, the Xanax was starting to kick in and she was able to make some inane conversation about the beautiful grounds outside and how pretty everything was, and then added that she would be starting on the portrait shortly, as soon as she was able to take the photos.

"I'll go get my better half and we'll be right back," Cindy said as she spun around in her chair and headed back out to the main floor.

Outside, Allison was paying especially close attention to the guitar player. He must have been about her age, maybe a little older, and he was SO adorable. She was determined to watch him play every song. "Jamie," she began, "I'm going to stay here and watch the band. Can you go and find Dobs and Nikki and let them know where I'll be?"

"Can I watch with you?" Jamie asked.

"Maybe. Sure, why not? Go let them know what we are doing. And bring back a plate of food and a drink to share, if it looks good. We can eat out here."

The guitar player kept looking over towards Allison as he tuned his guitar. Once the band started playing, he looked her way as she and Jamie ate their lunch from a paper plate and shared from the same paper cup of soda. They played mostly older songs, which was fine with Allison. And they did a great job, especially on Elton John's *Your Song.* When the band finally took a break, he walked over to where they were sitting.

CHAPTER 22

"Hi, my name is Joe. Are you girls enjoying yourself?" He was much cuter up close and Allison felt it all over. Her face felt flushed and her legs were almost trembling as she spoke.

"You guys are so good!" This was all she was able to say.

"Thank you. Like I said, my name is Joe."

"Her name is Allison, but you can call her Alli. And I'm Jamie." Jamie spoke up, realizing Allison was having a hard time. "Are you guys from around here?"

"Yeah," Joe answered. "We go to Valor." Valor was a large Christian based private school in Highlands Ranch, known mostly for how much the campus looked like a modern day Hogwarts out of the Harry Potter movies. Allison knew this meant that they all came from money. She had heard the tuition at Valor was $1,000 a month. Dobs had asked her if she wanted to go there instead of the public high school but she had said no.

"Valor,wow!" Allison said. "I go to Highlands Ranch and Jamie here goes to Cresthill Middle." Allison paused before looking right into his eyes. "You really are very good with that guitar. And your voice is great. We are so totally impressed."

Joe looked at Alli. "So, do you sing?"

"Well, actually, I do a little."

"She is really very good," said Jamie. "Let her sing a song with you guys, come on. She's really good. I promise."

Joe was still looking at Allison. "What do you say, Alli?"

Allison knew she could handle it but was still trembling from how she felt about Joe. "Do you guys know any Fleetwood Mac?" She knew them from Nikki playing them all the time.

"Sure do." Joe replied. "Yeah, actually, we did play Gold Dust Woman for a school function last year. Can you sing it?"

"Let's find out." Allison stood up and followed Joe up on to the stage where he gave her a microphone and told the rest of the band what they were doing. When Allison sang the chorus of the song for the third time, over half of the guests were standing and listening to her. Her voice was so rich and melodic as it radiated through the rock formations surrounding them. In the back of the crowd, Andrea had emerged from her work area and was also standing there listening to the song, much too far away from the stage to realize it was her daughter singing.

After a warm round of applause, Allison left the stage and rejoined Jamie next to the stage. She could tell Joe had been impressed and she knew she would be seeing him again on the next break.

Meanwhile, down at the outdoor dining area, Nikki and Dobs sat a few tables away from Cindy and her groom. Nikki had tears in her eyes from Allison's performance while Dobs tried to hide his. "So," he began, "did you have any idea she could sing like that?"

"Of course I did. I tried to encourage her singing last year but she had a bad experience with a music teacher at her old high school and he kind of ruined things for her."

"What kind of bad experience?" Dobs asked.

Nikki leaned over and told him about how Allison's music teacher had fondled her under her blouse, telling her he was just trying to feel the diaphragm vibrate while she sang. She ran out of the music class and never returned. But she still sang at home sometimes, especially when she was alone. Nikki explained all of this to Dobs softly so that none of the other guests at their table had any idea what had been said. They then continued with the table-wide small talk and finished their meal.

Many other couples had also finished eating and were now dancing to the music of the band. Cindy sat in her wheelchair with her husband sitting next to her as she smiled and watched the dancing while tapping her hand on the arm of the chair.

Nikki nudged Dobs to look over at Cindy and softly said in his ear, for a moment forgetting her own condition, "How sad is that?"

While the dancing and celebration continued outdoors, Andrea was busy inside the clubhouse trying to finish the portrait, softly singing part of the words to the Fleetwood Mac song she had just heard that wonderful girl sing.

She was about two thirds of the way done with the portrait and was currently working on the bride's face. As she painted, what had once been the face of Cindy slowly grew into the face of Allison. Oblivious to the change that was taking place, Andrea kept on painting and singing under her breath. She wasn't distracted from her work until she heard someone enter the room through a door behind her. Turning around casually, she saw that it was the bride and groom.

"What the hell?" said the groom. "What are you doing to her face?"

Andrea was startled and looked back at the portrait and realized what she was unconsciously doing. "Oh, not to worry. I always put the face of my beautiful darling daughter in as the bride's face before I finish my work. Now, run along you two. You shouldn't be seeing this yet anyway. It will be complete within the hour and you will love it!" She thought she had saved the situation with her quick and somewhat reasonable response.

"That's not your daughter's face," yelled Cindy. "That's the young girl who was just out there singing on stage." Cindy spun around in her chair and left the room, followed by her new husband.

Andrea sat in quiet desperation as she tried to grasp what had just been said. The girl outside singing had been Allison? How could that be? Allison was singing at the wedding while she sat in this room and painted the portrait. Well, I suppose it could have been her, she thought to herself, now feeling more rational as she slipped another Xanax under her tongue.

Andrea quickly changed the face in the portrait back to Cindy's face and made a few more broad strokes with the brush before she stood up to look at her creation. "Yes, it is perfect!" she said aloud as she began to clean off her brush and pack away her things. "And they are lucky to have had me do it for them."

Once she had everything packed away and had taken it out to her car, she came back to the clubhouse and walked over to a buffet table and grabbed a plate. She picked up a few hors d'oeuvres and cookies and began to walk towards the garden area, where she still heard the band playing. The stage was set up against the backdrop of the large red rock formations in the distance. But it was still too far away for her to see very much. Just as she began to step out into the patio area she came face to face with Dobs. Nikki was sitting in her wheelchair next to him. "What are you doing here?" His voice was gruff.

Ruffled somewhat by the surprise, Andrea countered, "I'm working here, what are you doing here?"

"We were invited," Dobs said, glaring at her.

"Well, I did the wedding portrait for the bride and groom. Is Allison here?" She asked nervously. "Is she outside? Was that her singing a while ago?"

Dobs reached into his jacket and pulled out his cell phone. "I still have Detective Boyle on speed dial."

"Oh yes, Detective Boyle. Well, I am here legally. My probation officer knows I am here."

"To do the painting, correct?"

"Right," Andrea answered, looking nervously over his shoulder towards the stage area about fifty yards away.

"So you are not here to see Allison, right?"

"That's right. But should I just happen to run into her I don't see any harm in that. Really, do you?"

"Listen to me. I know you had something to do with putting Nikki into this wheelchair. So, pack up your shit and get out of here. Now, or I call Boyle and tell him you're stalking Allison again." Dobs had a serious and even somewhat frightening expression on his face as he spoke.

"Okay, okay. I'm leaving. I fly back to Phoenix later today. I just wanted to see her and say hello." Looking disappointed Andrea was looking directly at Dobs. She had barely even looked towards Nikki.

Nikki said to her firmly, "Right now. Please leave."

Andrea turned and walked back towards the parking lot, just as the band began to play again.

"So now she knows we live here. What do we do? Go back to California?" Nikki started to cry from the stress of the surprise encounter with Andrea. "What are we supposed to do?"

"Wait here." Dobs walked out towards the parking lot just in time to see Andrea pull away.

When he returned to Nikki's side he said, "She's gone. And she has no idea where we live. So do you want to stay for a while and try to enjoy ourselves? She is on her way back to Phoenix. I'll have Boyle call her parole officer and let him know we ran into her. It could have happened anywhere since they let her travel around like that. Come on. Let's get a drink and enjoy the party."

The rest of the afternoon was not the opportunity Dobs and Nikki had thought it might be to make new friends, but they were able to have somewhat of a good time. Not as much of a good time as Allison was having making plans to see Joe later that night, on her first real date.

Andrea had checked out of her hotel earlier that day, before going to the wedding, and her flight was not until four-thirty. She still had an hour or two. Her rental car's navigational system had her driving right by Highlands

Ranch High School fifteen minutes after she left the country club.

She pulled into the school parking lot, which was empty because it was Saturday, and parked her car. She stared out at the front of the school and thought about how wonderful it would be if she were really going to be Allison's mother. But she knew she wasn't going to be. Not anymore. She would leave her alone and let her grow up with Nikki and Dobs. She would go back to Phoenix and concentrate on her painting. Then, maybe, if she made enough money at it, she could offer to pay for Allison's college. Maybe then they would let her see her, every now and then.

Of course, Allison wouldn't even need their permission when she turned eighteen. She could just come live with her if she wanted to, maybe even go to Arizona State in Phoenix. Andrea wondered about what Allison would want to be when she grew up. Maybe if she wrote her a letter and sent it to her attention at the high school, they could begin a correspondence. Then she could hear all about Allison's high school adventures, her loves and heartbreaks, maybe even find out what she might want to study in college. If Andrea could just leave it all alone now and fly back to Phoenix at four-thirty, things might actually work out after all.

Andrea stared at the front entrance of the school and tried to imagine her smiling daughter walking out the door and walking towards her car to greet her with a big hug. She began to cry as she started the car and backed out of the parking space, aware that no one was walking out to see her. She programmed Denver International

Airport into the car's navigation system and followed the directions, singing what few words she knew to Gold Dust Woman as she drove away. She remembered something about "Did she make you cry? Make you break down? Shatter your illusions of love. Now tell me is it over now - do you know how - to pick up the pieces and go home?"

Tears fell down her cheeks as she remembered hearing Allison sing the song. If only she could have seen her, somehow gotten closer to the stage. But it didn't matter now. She saw her singing when she closed her eyes. She heard her sing "Rock on Ancient Queen" and wondered if she was singing the song to her.

Andrea flew home on the four thirty flight to Phoenix. When she got back to her house the lights were on inside, although they were dim. The timer was working again. After unpacking and taking a quick shower, she poured herself a glass of Chardonnay and walked over to the cabinet that held her CD player and speakers. She reached into the cabinet and pulled out the Fleetwood Mac Rumors CD she hadn't listened to in years and put it into the player. After turning up the volume loudly and choosing the Gold Dust Woman track to play, she walked over and cracked a window that opened on to her patio. She walked outside on to the deck and sat down with her glass of wine to listen to the song. "Yes," she said out loud. "She was singing that song to me."

Epilogue

A full year passed without hearing from Andrea. Dobs, Nikki, Allison, and Jamie spent that year in Colorado before returning to their home in California. Paul had taken very good care of Nikki's house and when she called him to let him know they were moving back he sounded excited. He told her he had missed working with her and hoped they would be working together again very soon. He told her the fitness studio was still doing very well and that he thought the physical therapy addition was still a great idea. Dobs put his Huntington Beach condo, which he had rented out while he was gone, up for sale and moved in to Nikki's house.

They were planning on getting married in June of 2013, only nine months away. Nikki had made great progress but still used the wheelchair. She could walk across the room and fall into his arms, which was a totally unexpected but much appreciated improvement, after a year and a half of physical therapy and stem cell injections. The clinic she had gone to in Colorado was wonderful but she really was happy to be back in California, back in her own home.

Dobs had only seen his daughter and son-in-law twice in Colorado. Now that his son-in-law was stationed in Yemen, where our latest war raged on, Dobs was looking forward to seeing a lot more of Dawn. Hopefully she would even stay with them while Tim was away.

Allison transferred back to Laguna Beach High School and loved it. Jamie was a freshman now so they got to attend the same school and Allison was even able to drive them to school now that she had a license and her own car. School started on August 23, just a few weeks after they got back.

It looked like Sarah Palin would definitely be the next president. The election was only a few months away. She and her running mate, Michelle Bachman, had successfully beaten Romney in the primaries and were far ahead of Obama in the polls. The economy had never really recovered and jobs were the big issue now. Jobs and the never ending war on terror.

Palin was convinced that the country needed to fight terrorism wherever it reared its head. Unfortunately, that was all over the place. So we now had troops in Yemen, Libya, Afghanistan, Pakistan, Somalia, and 50,000 still in Iraq. Palin had already discussed bringing back the draft. Dawn's husband, Tim, was a Lance Corporal Tow Gunner in Yemen. He had been over there a few months.

Dobs had contacted the private investigator, Scott Fletcher, when they first got back and asked him to check to see if Andrea was still in Phoenix. Dobs wanted to avoid any surprises. After a few days, Scott reported back to Dobs that indeed Andrea was still in Phoenix and was spending most of her time campaigning for the Palin for President ticket, when she wasn't busy doing a portrait. She had lost her right to vote but felt so strongly about Sarah that she wanted everyone else to vote for her. Which was great news for Dobs. Perhaps this meant she had found a new calling in life and would be leaving Allison alone from now on.

Dobs was sitting on the side deck and Nikki was sitting in her chair by his side when he told her the news about Andrea. Nikki took a sip of her hot tea before saying, "One can only hope, Dobs. One can only pray."

Dobs sat silently, contemplating how bizarre a Palin presidency would be. And then it came to him. An idea for a new screenplay: *Andrea Goes to Washington.* He smiled as he said out loud, "It might work!"

"What might work?" Nikki asked.

When he told her about his idea, they both laughed together before Nikki stopped laughing and looked right into his eyes very seriously and said, "Listen to me, Mr. Dobson, that movie is over. Got it?"

"Yeah," Dobs looked into her eyes and knew it was a really bad idea. "I get it. It's over. And I love you."

"I love you too."

ABOUT THE AUTHOR

Frank Drury is the author of AN EMPTY SKY, published in 2010. Midwest Book Review called it “a fascinating and thought provoking read”. He spent the early years of his career as a struggling screenwriter in California before moving to the East Coast and finding success in the high risk world of futures trading, which is where he gained the inspiration for AN EMPTY SKY. He currently lives in Highlands Ranch, Colorado with his wife and daughters and continues to write fiction. A DREAM AWAY is his latest novel. His books are available through Kindle, Amazon.com, BarnesandNoble.com, Booksamillion.com, Powell’s Books, Tattered Cover, and Boulder Bookstore. It may also be purchased through your local independent book store. You may contact the author at frankdrury@gmail.com

Made in United States
North Haven, CT
22 January 2024

47738719R00139